CHAPTER 1

She stepped off the small boat, her heeled ankle boot digging into the wet sand. What a metaphor for her life. Walking into what was supposed to be a great new job opportunity, and she was already sinking. *Just great.*

"Here, let me help you, ma'am," the young man said as he jumped off the boat and grabbed her hand, steadying her before she walked right out of her brand new shoes. Why she had worn such an expensive pair was beyond her, but then again, she wasn't exactly thinking clearly these days.

She reached up and grabbed her large brim sun hat, trying to hold it to her head as the wind whipped around her. Who knew coastal South Carolina was this windy? She'd been to Chicago once as a kid and thought she might get swept into the sky like Dorothy from The Wizard Of Oz, but this seemed more forceful. Of course, what could she expect from an island?

"I guess I thought there'd be a dock of some kind,"

she shouted over the sound of the gusts. The wind whistled around her, sounding like a ghostly choir. Not a great omen.

"Sorry 'bout that. We have a small dock on the other side of the island, but the boat was a little lower on gas than I thought," the young man said sheepishly, his southern accent thicker than most she'd heard. Having been raised in Atlanta, she'd heard plenty of accents, but she'd tried to rid herself of hers a long time ago.

"No problem," she muttered, just wanting to make it to the concrete parking lot she saw up the hill. He continued holding her arm until they made it there, and she kicked off her boots so she could tap them together and get rid of the sand that had already accumulated inside. Meanwhile, Jeremy - the boat driver whose name she'd just remembered - ran back to fetch her luggage. Poor guy could barely carry it all in one trip.

He gingerly set it all down and blew out a breath. "You sure carry a lot of stuff, ma'am," he said, forcing a smile, his chubby face red from exertion. She felt kind of bad. Kind of.

"Sorry. Here's a little extra something for your troubles." She tried to hand him five dollars, but he shook his head and held up his hand.

"We don't do that around here, ma'am."

"Do what?"

"Accept tips."

She stared at him, her eyebrows furrowed together in confusion. "And why is that?"

"We believe in just helping each other. Kindness doesn't cost a thing."

She smiled. "That sounds nice, Jeremy, but a man's got to eat, right?" She slid the bill into his shirt pocket.

"Thanks anyway, ma'am," he said, returning it to her hand.

Before she had the chance to try again, a man in a golf cart came screeching around the corner, almost toppling it over as he tried to avoid her luggage piled high beside her.

"Well, you must be Dani!" he said with a larger-than-life laugh. The man was grossly overweight and way too big to be occupying the small golf cart. His hair, a mixture of black and silver with not much on top, was sticking out every direction, as if he'd never seen a hairbrush. He wore a short sleeve white dress shirt, the buttons stretched to their maximum capacity over his expansive belly. Khaki shorts, riding low below said belly, topped off the ensemble. Oh, and how could she forget the baby blue boat shoes that adorned his wide feet?

"Danielle," she corrected, reaching out her well-manicured hand. If there was something her mother had taught her, it was to always have a good manicurist. Sally had served her well over the years, and she hoped to find someone on the island who would do as good a job.

"That's a little formal for these parts," he said, stepping out of the golf cart with a grunt loud enough to hear over the winds. She hoped it wasn't this windy every day.

"And you are?"

"I'm Eddie. I guess you might call me Edward, but I sure wouldn't answer to it!" He laughed loudly at his own joke and then coughed to catch his breath. She leaned back, unsure of what germs he might spew at her, although the wind would quickly carry anything away.

Being raised with two doctors as parents had given her way too much information about viruses and bacteria. Her mother, a noted epidemiologist, had worked at the Centers for Disease Control in Atlanta for almost a decade before moving to New York City for more hands-on work at a research lab. Her father, before their big, ugly divorce, had been a neurosurgeon specializing in hard to treat brain tumors before dying of one himself six years ago. Irony wasn't always funny.

"Nice to meet you, Eddie," she said, as Jeremy quickly loaded her luggage onto the back of the golf cart. After seeing Eddie's driving capabilities, she wondered how it would stay on without flying off into the tornado-like winds. Surely, some dolphin would use her make-up bag as a flotation device before long.

His hand, both sweaty and sticky at the same time, enveloped hers. She'd been petite her whole life, relegated to the top position of the pyramid in cheerleading and always the one everybody wanted to pick up like some kind of baby. Being only five foot two meant always needing a step stool and working hard to get anyone to take her seriously. After the year she'd had, her reputation was of great importance to her.

This job would give her the opportunity to rebuild her life, if that was even possible.

"Hop on! I'll take you over to your cottage." He wiggled his big body back behind the steering wheel, much to Danielle's amazement. One button, already barely hanging on, finally popped open, his hairy belly button region on full display. She sat down next to him, her head turned so she wouldn't see *that* again. "Hang on!"

As they zipped down the small streets, the first thing Danielle noticed was how clean this place was. There were no trash bins on the streets, if they could even be called streets. They were more like paved pathways, only large enough for golf carts and bicycles. Of course, there were no cars here, and certainly no easy way to get one to the island.

At just over five-thousand acres, the small island had been uninhabited and undeveloped until three years ago when a very wealthy tech entrepreneur had come up with an idea that seemed crazy at the time. The media had a field day with it, from what Danielle found while doing her research. Of course, she'd been busy working at the hospital, so she had paid little attention to the news back then.

Now, here she was, zipping around the island and wondering if she'd made the right choice. After all, it wasn't like she didn't have choices. None of them had allowed her to disappear from her problems like this one would.

"Your place is just around this bend," he said,

reaching his arm across her chest, being careful not to actually touch her. "Hang on!" he repeated.

She reached up and held onto a bar that stretched across the ceiling of the golf cart, not wanting to reach forward and have this strange man's hands on her breasts. That wouldn't have been a great way to start her first day.

Without warning, he slammed on the brakes, coming to a screeching halt in front of a small cottage. The first word that popped into her mind was "weathered", although that was being kind. It reminded her of when her mother had gone through that farmhouse phase, redecorating everything in their kitchen to look old and worn, even though they lived in one of the most expensive neighborhoods in Atlanta. Of course, it didn't last. Before long, she was replacing everything with ornate gold frames and crystal chandeliers.

This little place was truly weathered, and she didn't understand. Everything else in sight was brand new, with bright white or yellow paint. In fact, it all looked like a movie set from the nineteen-fifties. She fully expected to see a milkman delivering on the street at any moment.

Not surprisingly, there was also wisteria everywhere, planted in yards and sometimes running up the sides of buildings. The island was awash in purple.

"Um, I don't mean to be ungrateful, but..." she said slowly as Eddie slid out of the cart.

"Yeah, she needs some fixin', but her bones are good."

"Her bones?"

"The original owner of this island, a Mr. Herman Lanafort, built this house for himself and his mistress back in nineteen-hundred and twenty-eight."

"His mistress?"

"As the story goes, Mr. Lanafort was very rich. He had a mansion in Atlanta somewhere, but he bought this island to spend some... quality time... with his mistress, Roxy Lou."

Danielle stepped out of the cart and stood there, trying to decide between hijacking the golf cart to get back to the boat or forcing herself to stay in the abandoned hook-up shack.

"Roxy Lou?"

He leaned against the golf cart, his weight pushing it sideways a bit. "Legend has it that Roxy Lou was an exotic dancer." He said it so softly, as if Roxy Lou's family were living nearby and might beat him up. "Anyway, it all came to a tragic end in nineteen-twenty-nine when the market crashed and the Great Depression happened. Old Mr. Lanafort lost Roxy Lou to another rich man who *hadn't* lost all his money. He ended up jumping off a bridge somewhere in Atlanta, and his family inherited this island."

"Nobody wanted it?"

"Nope. They just kept it in the family until the current owner found out about it and bought it a few years back. And that's how this very unique place was born!" He held out his arms like he was a proud papa, showing her his new baby.

Trying to procrastinate about going into the rickety

little cottage, she continued asking questions. "What exactly do you do here, Eddie?"

"I'm the property manager. I used to live over on Hilton Head Island managing big condo complexes, but I enjoy this a lot more. It's really about the people, ya know?"

"I suppose so. How big is this island?" She knew the acreage, but that meant nothing to her in terms of how big it actually was.

"Only about six miles long and about three miles wide. We've got over five-thousand acres here, give or take."

"Right. And how many residents?"

"At the moment, we have about ninety-seven, although we've had as many as one-hundred twenty-five before. Given our age range, we lose a few from time to time," he said, softly, his face serious for a moment. "That's always hard."

"Of course."

"That's why you're here!"

"Well, I'm definitely hoping to make a difference, but I can't stop the hands of time."

He chuckled. "Sure. Well, let's get you settled in. Sun's about to set, so you'll want to get ready for dinner."

"Oh, I'm not really hungry. I usually skip dinner."

He stopped in his tracks, his eyes wide. "Oh, you have to eat dinner with the residents. It's part of the job."

She stared at him. "Part of the job?"

"I'm sure the boss man will explain it all tomorrow

when you meet. I guess it'd be okay for you to skip it tonight. Just don't tell anyone I said that."

She grabbed two of her smaller bags while Eddie took the others, and they headed for the front door. The porch, which had seen better days, spanned the front of the cottage. Maybe she could get the wood repaired and sealed so she'd feel comfortable sitting in a chair out there for her evening coffee. Right now, she felt like she might slip straight through the rotting wood and into the sand below.

Eddie opened the door, revealing a small, dark, musty space with furniture covered in drop cloths and tarps. She looked around, immediately regretting her decision to come to this godforsaken island.

"Wow," she said softly as they walked toward the back of the house. She set her bags on the kitchen counter, which seemed to be the only place not covered in dust or sand. The sound of her heels clapped against the floor, getting stuck in a hole along the way.

"Look at that view!" Eddie proclaimed when they got to the back window. It was a nice view, unobstructed all the way to the ocean. She could now see the dock that Jeremy had mentioned. There was a small boat tied up there, maybe the one she'd ridden in on, but she hadn't been paying close attention.

"Very nice. Listen, Eddie, this place isn't remotely livable."

Eddie turned to her and laughed, the sound echoing and bouncing around the room like a pinball. "Tell that to our last eight nurses!"

"Wait. They lived here? And you've had eight in the last three years?"

Eddie paused for a long moment, obviously wishing he could take back his previous sentence. He cleared his throat. "Well, yes, and yes. It's been a few months since anybody lived here, though, so I'm sure it just needs a little freshening up."

Danielle looked down at the floor, which was covered in at least a quarter inch of white sand. "Eight nurses? Why?"

"Well, living here has some wonderful advantages and also some unique challenges."

She puckered her lips and cocked her head to the side. "That was a party line statement if there ever was one. Tell me the actual truth, Eddie."

"Eddie? You in here?" The voice of an older woman permeated the cottage. Danielle turned to see her standing in the living room, her hands on her hips. She had to be in her eighties, but she was wearing a square dancing outfit and glittery tights, her hair dyed a pale pink and swept into a bun on top of her head.

"Oh, hey, Janice. This is Dani, our new nurse!"

"Danielle. It's nice to meet you," she said, reaching out her hand to shake Janice's.

"Oh, sugar, I don't shake hands. That's how you get germs, and I'm not ready to croak yet!"

Danielle drew her hand back and smiled. "That's quite an outfit."

Janice laughed and twirled around. "It's the square dancing championship tonight. I'll be darned if that old biddy, Mabel, is going to win again this season!"

"You have square dancing *seasons?*"

Janice laughed loudly. "Oh, you'll learn the ropes here soon enough! Say, Eddie, we need you over at the dance hall to call the dances. You're very late, you know?"

Eddie looked down at his watch. "Oh, man! I didn't know my watch stopped. I'll have to get a new battery when I'm back on the mainland again. Listen, Dani, can you settle in on your own for a bit? I'll check back with you after the championship, okay?"

He trotted toward the door, following Janice back onto the sidewalk. "Wait! What am I supposed to do here?" she called as they hurried to the golf cart.

Eddie just waved as they rounded the corner, Janice's little pink bun bobbing in the breeze.

What had she done? She turned back toward the cottage and walked inside, all the while wondering if she could possibly hot-wire the boat out back and get the heck out of this crazy place.

No amount of cleaning was going to do it, she decided. As she wiped her brow with the back of her hand, she imagined herself standing in her old condo, all shiny and clean after the housekeeper left. The sparkling jetted tub. The shiny granite countertops in the kitchen. The hardwood floors that glistened in the bright light of the beautiful dining room fixture. Very unlike the beat-up wood floor beneath her feet right now that felt as if it would cave in at any moment.

What had she done to her life? Just a year ago, it was all so different. She'd been at the top in her field, running the ICU unit at the best hospital in Atlanta. Working alongside her fiancé, a doctor in the same ICU, her life had been right on track.

Sure, her mother had encouraged her to accept Richard's proposal even though she'd had second thoughts the moment she'd said yes. She'd been dating him for almost two years, after all. It wasn't like it was a rushed thing, but something had never felt quite right. That internal feeling she'd thought she would have when she met the love of her life just wasn't there.

As her mother reminded her at the time, she wasn't getting any younger. Almost forty years old, she had always assumed her life would be different. Instead, her career had gotten the better of her, and before she knew it, all of her girlfriends were married with kids in middle and high school, and she was still dating IV drip bags and heart monitors.

But this whole fiasco of an idea took the cake.

How had she found herself in this mess? No fancy job. No fiancé. And way too much embarrassment to ever go back to Atlanta or any of the surrounding areas. She could never show her face there again.

No, this was her punishment for being so stupid. So trusting. So gullible. She'd live out her days on an island of old folks, eating pea soup and square dancing. Living in her shack. Waving at the passing dolphins, who would laugh at her with their little dolphin friends.

Danielle sank down into the plastic Adirondack

chair on the rickety deck overlooking the vast expanse of ocean and sighed. It was a deep sigh, like it came from the pit of her soul.

She closed her eyes and tried to remember what life was like even six months ago. It seemed like a lifetime ago, and she longed to go back to that place of normalcy before everything became so very abnormal. Even though she'd been exhausted by her hectic schedule, she knew how to live that life. How to exist on takeout Chinese food from Golden Dragon. How to interact with patients and their families during the worst times of their lives. How to detach herself from feeling things she didn't want to feel.

Maybe that was why she'd been so ready to get married to a man she didn't really love because feeling things too deeply was dangerous. Richard allowed her to avoid getting in too deep. They were both focused on their careers, and it was a good match. A good compromise. A good partnership. Until it wasn't.

CHAPTER 2

There wasn't much that Bennett Alexander hated more than meeting with new nurses for the island. So many had come and gone over the last three years that he almost hated to go through the trouble of explaining the position and the rules of living on Wisteria Island.

His brainchild, the unique community had been on his mind for years before the island had come up for sale. It had provided the perfect opportunity to create his vision, but some days he wondered if he'd made the right decision.

Wealthier than most people could ever imagine, he would soon hit forty-five years old with more in his bank account than he could ever need. That didn't mean he had everything he wanted. He tried not to let those thoughts creep in, though.

"Mr. Alexander? The new nurse is here," his assistant Naomi said, popping her head through his doorway. Naomi had been with him for seven years, moving from the big high-rise office building he'd owned in Boston to the tiny South Carolina island. It had been quite a culture shock for them both.

"Thanks. You can send her in." He looked down at the file on his desk. Danielle Wright was her name. He knew little else about her since the staffing agency had done all the legwork. Moments later, she walked through the door. Bennett was surprised at how petite she was. He hoped she was strong enough to handle the physical nature of the job.

"You must be Mr. Alexander?" she said, smiling. He stood and reached out his hand.

"Please, call me Bennett. Have a seat."

She sat down and cleared her throat. "Very nice office." She looked around and then back at him, her jaw clenching a bit.

"Thanks." She stared at him like the cat that ate the canary. "Why do I get the feeling you have something on your mind, Miss Wright?"

"Well, I'm just a little surprised at how nice so many of the buildings are on this island… except the place where you want your nurse to live."

He smiled slightly. "Not the first time I've heard that."

"And yet you have done nothing about it?"

Bennett chuckled. "We're getting off to quite a start…"

"Look, I don't mean any disrespect, but I have to say that sleeping in that ramshackle cottage last night not only gave me a crick in my neck, but may have also resulted in me getting up on the wrong side of the bed.

So, unless you'd like for me to invent new types of mold and mildew, I don't understand the point of putting me there."

She had gumption, he'd give her that. "I have to admit that I haven't seen the inside of the cabin since I bought the island."

Her eyes widened. "You *really* should see it then. It's the stuff nightmares are made of."

"I'll make a point of that," he said, jotting it down on his ever-growing to-do list. Weren't wealthy people supposed to sit back and eat expensive chocolates all day? Because his life certainly wasn't going that way.

"Thank you."

She definitely seemed a little rough around the edges, like a scalded dog. He probably shouldn't say that out loud. No woman would appreciate being compared to a dog. She certainly wasn't a dog with her cute button nose and her... Never mind, he thought to himself. He came to this island to get away from attractive women, and he sure would not pursue an employee of his.

"So, I wanted to go over your job description, duties, rules of the island, and so forth. How much do you know about Wisteria Island?"

"Very little." Well, at least she was honest.

"Wisteria Island is a retirement village for those over sixty, and some might even refer to us as semi-assisted living. We have some residents who are fully independent and others who need more support, which is where you come in. We are not a typical assisted living center or a nursing home, so our residents are mostly healthy people."

"Why do people move here?"

"To tell you the truth, many of our residents don't have supportive family."

"That's awful. I ran across that a lot when I worked in a hospital setting. Some people would never get visitors, and they would die alone."

"We consider everyone here to be family to us. Many of them were put here by family who didn't want the responsibility. Others came on their own because they could afford it, and let's face it - Wisteria Island is a beautiful place to live."

She scrunched her nose. "Well, for most people."

"I promise I will come look at that cottage," he said, smiling. "So, back to what I was saying... As you can see, you can only access the island by boat, so it was important to make this a freestanding city all on its own. Each resident has a job, and they earn tickets instead of money. They use those tickets for many things including golf, our spa, workout classes, the movie theater..."

"Wait. There's a movie theater and a spa?"

"I told you, it's just like any other town. We have a grocery store, a beauty salon, coffee shop, drive-in theater for golf carts, a bakery and a lot more."

"Sounds like you've built the perfect city."

He smiled. "I like to think so."

"Do families come for visits?"

"We have scheduled family visits once per quarter. Loved ones come and visit for a few days. Otherwise, there are a lot of video calls for those who have interaction with family. Of course, residents can also travel to visit family, but that rarely happens for most of them. All of our employees live on the island too."

"So, how will I factor in when it comes to medical care?"

He stood up and sat on the edge of his desk. "Your role is very important. You are the primary medical support residents have here. We have a doctor on the mainland that comes once a month for any pressing issues, but aside from that, you will be tasked with taking care of our residents. Everything from sprained ankles to high blood pressure. You'll pretty much always be on-call, although most residents are in bed fairly early."

"I have to ask this. If this place is such a utopia, why have so many nurses left?"

Bennett sighed. "I'll be honest with you, Miss Wright," he said, almost laughing when he said her name. Miss Wright? Was the universe making a joke? "The residents here are unique. Some are more difficult than others. A few of them delight in creating drama. Remember, many are outcasts from their own families, but they become our family no matter what. We don't give up on anyone. I just hope you have a thick skin because I really don't want to have to hire another nurse."

"Why are you doing this? Surely it's not a big money-making venture for you?"

"I do all right. This place was never about making money. My grandmother - her name was Della - was my idol. I adored her. We were quite poor when I was a kid, and when it came time that we couldn't care for her anymore, my mother put her in the local nursing home. I'll never forget how sad she was there. I hated going there to visit her. There was this smell - a mixture of orange scented cleaner and nasty cafeteria food. It would just turn your stomach. Anyway, the place was state run, and it got shut down after she died. I just remember thinking how horrible it was for people to live their entire lives and then end up in a place like that. So, when I started making money, I began planning Wisteria Island. My grandmother loved wisteria, hence the name."

He sensed her expression softening a bit. "That's a great story, Mr. Alexander."

"Please, call me Bennett."

"Okay, Bennett," she said, smiling as she stood up. "And you can call me Danielle."

"I'll try to remember that." Why did this conversation feel like it was bordering on flirtatious? Maybe it was because he never left the island much, and he really needed to go on a date soon.

"Any other questions?" he said, getting back behind his desk for safety.

"Oh, just one. Eddie said I need to have dinner with the residents?"

"Yes. That's one of our rules."

"And why is that?"

"Listen, Danielle, you're going to need to socialize with these people to gain their trust. You have no idea how untrusting some of them can be. Dinner is a part of that. Get out into the community. Visit the stores, spend some time looking around and getting to know people. They need you more than they realize."

She nodded. "Will do." As she walked toward the door, she turned back. "Are you coming to my place later?"

Bennett froze for a moment. "What?"

"That place will not fix itself, so unless you have an old-man construction crew, I assume you're Mr. Fix It?"

He let out the breath he'd been holding. "I'll tell ya what. I'll come by after dinner and take a look."

She smiled slightly. "Bring a toolbox."

As Bennett watched her walk away, he wondered if Wisteria Island was ready for her. Or maybe he was more worried about himself.

As DANIELLE STOOD outside of the cafeteria, her hands felt a little sweaty. It was never becoming for a woman to have sweaty hands, but it was her one cue that anxiety was lurking in her body. As a former ICU nurse, sweaty hands weren't something she often experienced. The high level of stress and pressure in her former workplace was something she thrived on, and she rarely felt anxious about anything. Well, until the end, when she had to leave her job. That was pretty stressful.

She shook her head in an effort to rid herself of the terrible memories from that time in her life. This was her new beginning, as odd as it was. She had to make the best of it. There were no other choices at this point.

Forcing a smile, she pushed the swinging door open and took in the scene before her. The place was decked out like a real fifties diner, complete with black and white checkerboard floors, a long chrome bar, fake red leather bar stools, and small square tables scattered across the enormous room. A jukebox played fifties tunes from the other side of the room, its lights alternating a glow of pink and orange.

This wasn't at all what she'd expected. Instead of a dingy hospital-style cafeteria, she'd literally walked into a party where people were laughing, eating and even dancing.

"Welcome to dinner, Dani girl!" Eddie said as he walked up and lightly slapped her on the shoulder. He was drinking a beer, which was odd all by itself, but he was also wearing a Hawaiian shirt and a plastic lei. She wondered what his closet looked like. It was most certainly colorful, probably like a box of Crayons had exploded.

"Danielle. And why are you wearing that?"

"It's Hawaiian night!" he said, pretending to do the hula. One more beer and she feared Eddie would fall face-down in the large vat of pudding on the buffet next to them.

"I must've missed that memo," she said dryly, trying to stay open-minded. She wasn't one for theme nights or dressing up in crazy costumes. Even as a kid, she didn't understand the point of Halloween. If you could buy candy at the store without all the work of dressing up, why not just do that? Then again, she'd always been a practical sort. It had served her well in her nursing career.

"Come on over here. I want to introduce you to a few of the residents," Eddie said, a big grin on his face. He had more energy than most people she'd met in her life.

"Sure," she said as she followed him over to the bar stool area. Danielle had to admit that she'd never seen a group so incredibly lively and eclectic. In fact, it was hard to take in all the crazy outfits, music and general noise going on in the diner. Some people were eating, others were dancing, and Danielle wasn't sure exactly what to do with herself.

"Dani, I want you to meet one of our longest residents. This is Hazel Hastings."

The older woman was a sight to behold with her pink poodle skirt and pony tail pulled on top of her head. Danielle couldn't guess her age, although she assumed it was a pretty high number.

"Nice to meet you, Hazel," she said, reaching out her hand. Hazel looked down at her hand and then back at Danielle.

"I don't shake hands with new people."

"Oh. Okay…"

Eddie chuckled. "Miss Hazel is a bit of a germaphobe. She'll shake your hand after you've been here a couple of weeks, right, Hazel?"

"We'll see," she said, shrugging her little shoulders before walking toward the jukebox.

"She's an interesting character," Danielle said,

unsure of what else to say. She'd never felt so much like a fish out of water as she did now.

"She'll warm up to you, eventually. You gotta understand, these people have seen more nurses than they ever wanted to see. You've got to prove yourself to them."

The only problem was that she wasn't sure she wanted to do that. This job was more involved than she realized. Sure, she'd had to have a personal relationship with her patients in the hospital, but she was in control there. They relied on her. They looked to her for guidance. Here, it seemed the inmates were in control of the asylum, so to speak.

"Dani, I'd like to introduce you to Mr. Mortimer Smith. We call him Morty."

The short man grinned like a Cheshire Cat and reached out his stubby little hand. "How do you do, madam?" he said flamboyantly as he bowed. Danielle shook his hand and forced a smile.

"Nice to meet you, Morty. I'm Danielle, the new nurse."

He waved both of his hands toward her. "Oh, Lordy be! Another nurse? Please tell me you have more staying power than the previous sourpusses Mr. Alexander hired!" Eddie joined him in laughter.

"Sourpusses?"

"They were simply no fun at all!" he said as he held his arms out and showcased his eye-catching outfit. He was wearing a rhinestone studded white suit with a matching cowboy hat, and Danielle wasn't sure she'd ever heard a thicker southern accent.

"I thought it was Hawaiian night?" Danielle whispered to Eddie.

"Morty does his own thing."

"I don't follow the crowd, darling," Morty said, obviously having heard her comment. She bit her lip in embarrassment. "Not all old people have hearing problems."

"I'm sorry. I'm just trying to learn how this place works," she said, trying to save face.

"It works because it allows each of us to be who we are. This is a family of outcasts, Miss Dani," Morty said. It had become apparent that no one would call her Danielle, no matter how many times she requested they did.

"Well, it was nice to meet you, Morty," she said, eager to move on.

"Nice to meet you, too. Dani, can I give you one piece of friendly advice?"

"Of course."

"Loosen up, dear. That face you're making will cause wrinkles."

As he trotted off to dance with a group of women, Danielle looked at Eddie. "I don't think he likes me."

Eddie shrugged his shoulders. "You need a thick skin here. They'll test you, for sure."

Oh, wonderful. What she needed was another test in her life. Why couldn't things just be easy? Life was always testing her.

Danielle spent the next hour going around the room with Eddie meeting different residents. Some were fairly nice, while others shot daggers with their eyes. It was obvious that they questioned her motives, and some simply didn't seem to like her. Maybe she was giving off the vibe she was actually feeling. Maybe they could see that she didn't want to be there. Maybe they could see she didn't want to be anywhere right now.

When they finally finished walking around, she was able to get a plate of food and sit down. She found an unoccupied table and plopped down, her feet killing her. The first chance she got, her new ankle boots were being flung into the ocean to be worn by a fashionable octopus.

"Mind if I sit?" She was surprised to look up and see Bennett standing there, a tray in his hand. More surprising was the vibrantly colored Hawaiian shirt he was wearing, along with a yellow and pink lei.

"Sure," she said, picking up her first bite of chicken casserole. It was surprisingly good.

"How's dinner going so far?"

"I don't think they like me very much."

He chuckled under his breath. "Well, to be fair, they've got some abandonment issues."

"How did the other nurses fare here?"

"Well, there was Kimber who stayed four hours total."

"Four hours?" She almost choked on her casserole. How bad was this place that someone only stayed four hours?

"And then there was Penelope, the lady from the UK. The residents couldn't understand her accent, and they got very offended when she wouldn't eat some of the southern food we serve here. She lasted six days…"

As Bennett rattled off facts about the previous nurses, Danielle became more and more uneasy. There was obviously something going on here that wasn't normal. Nurses were steadfast. Nurses were hard working. Nurses weren't quitters.

"You're scaring me."

He smiled. "I think you should know the truth, but I feel like you're tougher than some of the others we've hired before."

"Oh, really? And how do you know that?"

"Because you had no problem coming straight into my office and standing up for yourself. No other nurse has done that."

"And they've all lived in the shack?"

He laughed. "Yes, they've all lived in the *cottage*."

"I'm not sure this place is for me either, to be honest."

"Give it time. These people will grow on you if you give it a chance."

"They didn't grow on the other nurses," she said, taking a bite of her cornbread.

"Look, these people are my family, and I know some of them can be difficult. Did Hazel shake your hand?"

She chuckled under her breath. "No."

"Did Morty behave?"

She wasn't totally sure what that meant. "He told me I was going to get wrinkles because of the look on my face."

Danielle could tell Bennett was trying not to look at

her. "Morty is our resident life-of-the-party. You should see his closet."

"Yeah, he reminded me a bit of Liberace. My grandmother loved him with all of his fancy costumes and jewelry." She smiled to herself as she thought about her beloved Nana. There was no one in this world who'd loved her as much as her Nana, including her own mother. With Nana, there hadn't been requirements for her love. It was unconditional and without limits. She missed her every single day, even though she'd been gone for many years now. Nana would know what Danielle should do with her life, but there was no way to ask her now.

As she looked around the room, a part of her wondered if Nana would've liked a place like this rather than the assisted living home she'd lived in before she passed away. Even though Danielle visited her often, she still found it sad every time she went. So many residents would sit alone day after day, their own families too busy or uncaring to visit. The only family they knew were the workers in the facility.

"Where'd you go?" Bennett asked, waving his hand in front of her face.

"What?"

"You seemed lost in thought for a minute."

She smiled. "I was just wondering if my Nana would've liked a place like this."

"Ah. I see. As I told you, I created this place because of my grandmother."

"I have to say that I can see why. It's a good idea."

"You really think so?"

"In theory. I need to see it in action before I can issue any genuine compliments," she said, laughing.

"How's your food, by the way?"

"Not bad, actually. And yours?"

He looked down at his casserole. "The pot roast and meatloaf are my favorites, but this casserole is pretty good."

"Well, I hope it gives you plenty of strength and stamina."

"Why?"

"Because you're coming home with me."

He stared at her. "Excuse me?"

Realizing what she'd said, she coughed. "The cottage. Remember? You're coming to see the damage? And maybe fix some of it?"

"Oh, right. Of course."

Well, that dinner turned awkward really quickly.

CHAPTER 3

*B*ennett drove the golf cart toward the cottage, awkwardness still lingering between him and Danielle. How he'd misunderstood her at dinner was beyond him, but it certainly was embarrassing.

He pulled up in front of the cottage and immediately saw some of the damage she was talking about. The porch was in more disrepair than he'd realized, and he wondered why Eddie didn't tell him. That was a conversation for another day.

"Home sweet home," Danielle said dryly.

"Yeah, I see what you mean. I'm sorry I haven't checked on this more recently."

They stepped out of the golf cart and walked up to the front door. Danielle keyed the lock and opened it. As Bennett walked inside, he was shocked by the state of affairs. Dust and sand were everywhere. There were intermittent holes in the hardwood floors and some of the electrical outlets didn't seem to work.

"You can't stay here," he suddenly blurted out without thinking.

"What?"

"We have to find you another place. This place isn't habitable, and I'm sorry you had to sleep here last night."

Her face softened a bit. "That's unnecessary. It just needs some repairs."

"Well, until those repairs are done, let's find you another place to stay."

"Look, Bennett, I appreciate that, but I've already unpacked, so I'd rather stay here and get the repairs done."

She was one of the most adorably argumentative people he'd ever met. "Then stay with me for a couple of nights."

"What?" Her mouth dropped open and her already large eyes widened to a point where he thought they might just pop right out of her head.

"I didn't mean it that way…"

"Then what did you mean because it seems like my new boss just asked me to…"

"No!" he said, probably too loudly, before she could finish her sentence. "Your new boss wasn't asking you to do… that. I was offering my spare bedroom for a couple of nights until we can get our resident handyman to make some repairs."

She cleared her throat and averted his gaze. "I appreciate the offer, but I'm fine here until the repairs are done. Besides, I love my view."

"My house has a great view too, Danielle."

She smiled slightly. "I'm sure it does."

"Well, if you're sure about staying here, I'll head home now. I'll text Darryl, our handyman, and have him here first thing tomorrow."

"Thank you."

As he walked toward the door, he turned back. "Look, I know we've had a rough start here, but I hope you'll give this job a chance. I think you'll love it here if you just give it time."

"That's certainly my plan." He couldn't tell if she was being honest, but right now he just wanted to get out of there before he said something else stupid. Even though he hadn't meant to ask her to "sleep over" in the way she envisioned, he couldn't help but be attracted to her. There was just something about her that gave him shivers up his spine, and he wished that wasn't true.

Danielle woke up early the next morning after another fitful night of sleep. Trying to get comfortable in a totally new place on top of the horrible mattress they gave her was a challenge. She would make sure to have the handyman find a new mattress for her. As he hammered away on the front porch, she made a strong pot of coffee. If there was one thing working in a hospital had taught her, it was how to make coffee that would keep her awake until the next decade.

She padded across the kitchen, looking for anything to eat. There were some eggs in the fridge that were still in date from the last nurse, but she knew she'd have to visit the local grocery store on the island if she was going to have any chance of surviving this place. She found a small pad of paper and a pen and started making a list.

Once the coffee finished, she dug around in the cabinets until she found a mug that looked reasonably clean. Then she scrubbed it until she was satisfied it was sterile. Again, hospital training to the rescue. She poured a cup of the coffee - which looked more like liquified tar - and put it to her lips. Normally, she drank it with milk and a bit of stevia, but she had neither so straight it was.

Coughing after the first swallow, she continued drinking it. Something had to get her through this day. She was exhausted, both mentally and physically, and she was missing home. It really wasn't home anymore, anyway.

Still, she longed for her comfortable bed. It was king-sized with a top of the line mattress that even had a little remote control. She missed her jetted tub, her heated tile floors, her large walk-in closet full of clothes she never wore because her daily wardrobe had included scrubs at work and yoga pants and a t-shirt at home. She missed her cat, Scruffles, who she had to leave behind with her ex-fiance, Richard.

Richard.

Just hearing his name in her own head made her want to chuck the coffee mug across the room. Would it really matter, anyway? Darryl was here, and he could just add it to his list of holes to patch up.

Richard.

Again, his name pinged around her head like an unwelcome guest. She wanted to hate him, and she did. Sometimes. Other times, memories of their time together swept over her like a blanket, smothering her. She thought she'd loved him. Maybe she did. Her heart and mind were constantly at odds with the idea.

What he'd done to her was unforgivable, yet she had those good memories that were constantly antagonizing her, trying to convince her he was a good person. Flawed, but good. After all, he was a top-notch ICU doctor, and he'd saved countless lives in the years she'd known him. Didn't that make him inherently good?

As she pondered the imponderable, Darryl waddled into the kitchen. She shouldn't have thought of it as waddling, but Darryl was as wide as he was tall and his feet stuck out to the sides like a duck.

"Got the porch all patched up. Wanna take a look?"

"I trust you," she said. Truth was, she just wanted to drink her tar coffee and stare out the window at nothing while she internally stuck pins in a voodoo doll of her ex.

"Alrighty…" he said, sensing her disinterest. "I'll work on the holes in the living room floor then."

She nodded and poured herself another cup before walking toward her bedroom. "Oh, Darryl?"

"Yes, ma'am?"

Danielle scrunched her nose. "Ma'am? Ew, no. That makes me feel old. Just call me Danielle."

"Sorry, but we don't do that around here. Men are sir and women are ma'am."

She rolled her eyes. "Right. Well, anyway, I need a mattress that couldn't moonlight as a torture device. Where do I get one?"

He thought for a moment. "At the mattress store?"

Unsure if he was being sarcastic, Danielle pressed further. "I can't sleep on that thing. It's awful. A metal spring was poking me in the back all night, and I'm pretty sure a family of squirrels has taken up residence inside. So, unless you want me to burglarize someone's house tonight and steal their mattress right out from under them, please find me a mattress. Okay?"

He stared at her like he'd never heard a woman be so assertive. "Yes, ma'am. I'll find you something."

"Wonderful. Going to take a shower, so please stay at this end of the house."

Darryl nodded again, fear on his face. Good. She liked it when men were a little scared of her, especially now. No man was ever going to take advantage of her again. If it meant she had to be strong and domineering, she'd do it.

~

"No hummus?" Danielle asked the woman for a second time.

"Honey, we don't carry anything called hummus. What on earth is that?"

"It's used to dip vegetables or go on sandwiches. It's made of chickpeas, tahini…"

"Ta-what?"

"Tahini. Ground sesame seeds?"

The woman, who had to be in her seventies, cocked her head to the side like one of those little dogs who'd heard a loud noise. "We have mayonnaise."

"Yeah, it's not the same. But thanks anyway," Danielle said, pushing her cart in the other direction. This grocery store was as bare bones as it got. Only basic produce, things like apples, grapes and lettuce. Not an avocado in sight. Canned goods were more plentiful than anything else, probably because the manager focused on shelf-stable items. The only problem was that shelf-stable usually meant unhealthy, and that affected her and the people she would be treating. They needed more fresh produce, so she would add that to her list of things to discuss with Bennett.

"Danielle?"

Speak of the devil. "Hey, Bennett."

He pulled his cart closer to hers. "Stocking up on some groceries?"

She laughed. "I wouldn't call it stocking up. There's not a whole lot here."

"Seems to work okay for most of us," he said, shrugging his shoulders.

She peered into his cart. "You have ravioli, grapes and fruit roll-ups. Do you have kids?"

He chuckled. "Nope, just me."

"Bennett, this is not a healthy diet. I can't even get hummus here. We also need more fresh produce."

"It's just easier to get canned and boxed foods."

"Do you want these people to live longer? Have more vibrant lives?"

"Of course."

"Well, then we need to find fresh produce sources. How about a community garden? And maybe some classes about juicing and making green smoothies?"

"I'm not sure this demographic will be interested in that kind of thing."

"Don't stereotype," she said, wagging her finger at him. "People might be a lot more receptive than you think."

"I'll do some investigating and see what I can come up with. Meanwhile, how's it going with Darryl?"

"He fixed the porch and is working in the house now. I told him I desperately need a new mattress."

"I have an extra one in my guest room if you'd like to try it out?"

"Try it out?" She never could tell if her new boss was hitting on her. He was extremely good-looking, a fact that she tried to ignore. Richard had been handsome too, and look where that got her.

"To see if it's comfortable? I never have guests, so it hasn't been used. If you don't like it, we can order something else for you."

"Oh, okay. So I can just come by and check it out?"

"Absolutely. I'm busy today, but Naomi can meet you there."

"Naomi?"

"My assistant."

"Oh. Right. That sounds good."

He pulled a card from his pocket. "Here's my card. Naomi's cell is on here too. Just shoot her a text when you're ready and she can tell you how to get there."

She took the card and slipped it into her pocket. "Thanks."

"Well, I'd better finish my shopping."

"Yeah, be sure to get some cereal with the marsh-mallows in it," she said, smiling.

"Maybe you can teach me how to eat healthy too," he said, winking. Gosh, men who winked were often the cutest of all. She spun her cart around and started walking away.

"Goodbye, Bennett," she said, waving her hand behind her head.

As Danielle walked up to Bennett's house, she was amazed. Not because it was big and grandiose, because it wasn't. Not because it was fancy and expensive-looking, because it wasn't that either. Bennett's house was just as basic as hers, only it didn't need repairs. It was a small cottage on the opposite end of the beach.

"Danielle?" Naomi called, her head poking out of the front door.

"Thanks for meeting me," Danielle said as she walked up the three front steps.

"Come on in."

They walked inside, and it shocked Danielle to see just how simple Bennett lived. He was ultra wealthy, yet you would never know if magazines didn't harp about it all the time. He had a simple set of white canvas sofas, beach decor and basic artwork on the walls. No fancy rugs or expensive paintings. Just a nice, normal house.

"Wow. I guess I thought Bennett would have some giant mansion on the island."

Naomi laughed. "Bennett? No. He's the most down-to-earth guy I know. Comes from very basic means. Grew up poor, actually. He's not at all what the media portrays him to be."

"I see that."

"The guest room is this way," she said, pointing down a short hallway. The cottage was set up much like hers, with the kitchen on the right, the living room in the middle, and two small bedrooms down a hallway on the left. He also had a small glass enclosed sunroom on the back that overlooked the water.

As they walked down the hallway, she noticed the absence of personal pictures in the house. No framed photos of family or friends. In fact, his decorating taste was more minimalist than anything else, with lots of black and white and the occasional pop of blue to let you know he lived on the ocean. The sparseness of it made her feel a little sad, but she couldn't put her finger on why.

"Here we go," Naomi said as she opened the door to the guest room. It was painted a light gray and had white cottage-style furniture with a queen sized bed against the right wall. The floor, which was hardwoods, had a large jute rug that took up most of the space.

"Mind if I try it out?" Danielle asked, although at this point she'd take a bed of nails over what she currently had.

"Of course. Bennett insisted upon that."

She walked over and sat on the edge, bouncing up and down a bit. How did one try out a bed? Jump on it? Slide underneath the covers and wiggle around a bit? She didn't want to look like a weirdo, so she figured sitting on the edge and running her hand across it was sufficient.

"This should do quite nicely," she said as she stood back up. Naomi nodded.

"Excellent. I'll make arrangements for Eddie and Darryl to bring it over this evening. Will that work?"

"Yes, thank you."

They walked out of the room and back to the front door. "By the way, welcome to Wisteria Island."

"Thank you. It's an interesting place so far."

Naomi giggled. "Interesting is one way to put it."

"Can I ask you something?"

"Sure."

"Why does Bennett do this? I mean, he's a gazillion-aire. He could do or have anything. Why does he choose to be here with these older people and no social life?"

She looked taken aback a bit, but Danielle could tell she was trying not to show it. "Bennett is the most giving person I know. Money hasn't changed who he is at his core. To be honest, we all have our baggage. Wisteria Island is a great place to leave that baggage behind."

Danielle could understand that very well. Although she was curious about Bennett's baggage, it was probably best to leave that alone lest he want to know more about hers.

"Thanks for meeting me, Naomi."

"Can I drive you home?"

Danielle looked down the street. "No, thanks. I think I'll walk home and try to get more familiar with the island."

"Okay. Well, have fun!"

As Danielle walked down the stairs and started toward her house, she wondered what surprises awaited her on Wisteria Island. She had a feeling there was a lot more going on there than met the eye.

As Danielle walked along the road going back to the cottage, she looked around at all Wisteria Island offered. It really was something to marvel at, with its adorable buildings and clean streets. She passed the coffee shop, aptly named "Mugged", and then the salon, the bakery and what appeared to be the spa.

Many people she passed along the way said hello and waved. Some gave her dirty looks, while others whispered. She wondered what they thought of her and of the other nurses who had come before her and disappeared again.

As she neared her cottage, she saw a small pathway leading toward the beach. Maybe this would be a good time to go sit by the water and gather her thoughts. She started her office hours tomorrow, and the day would be a long one. After all, she had to set up her new office, figure out a filing system, and probably see at least a few patients.

Looking at her watch, she still had a few hours before dinner, so she figured it would be a good time to enjoy the ocean view. Although she could've just gone down to the water from her own beach, she decided to try this one and see if the view was different. The marsh was close by, so maybe she'd see some wildlife.

"Where are you headed?" a woman asked. She was standing at the edge of the sidewalk, her yappy little white dog on a leash. She definitely didn't seem to like that Danielle was there.

"Oh, sorry. Is this not a public access point to the beach?"

The woman stared at her like she'd lost her mind. "Yes…"

"I was just going to take in the view. I'm the new nurse here."

"Oh. I see."

"Just wanted to see some of the local beauty, maybe see something I haven't seen before."

The woman laughed under her breath. "Well, you'll definitely see that. It's a unique part of the beach, for sure. Have a good time."

As the woman walked away, Danielle got the distinct impression she was making fun of her. She decided it wasn't worth getting into an argument over and turned toward the beach.

She could feel the warm breeze as soon as she made her way between the two houses. There was just nothing like an ocean breeze to wash away the cares of the day. Well, maybe except for a bottle of wine. She'd washed many cares away with that. And chocolate. And a hot bath. Actually, wine with chocolate while taking a hot bath wasn't a bad way to wash away just about anything.

As she pondered the idea of having all three of those things later that night, she finally made it up onto the beach. She turned and looked to her right, toward her cottage, and saw very few people on the beach. One woman was sitting in a beach chair by the water, dipping her toes into the lapping waves. A man was walking further down with a metal detector, apparently looking for some treasures buried beneath the sand.

She wondered what the woman meant by it being a unique part of the beach. Nothing seemed particularly interesting here. On her left was a large stack of rocks that stretched from the house on her left, all the way to the water. Off in the distance, she could also see the marshland that surrounded part of the island. Maybe she should take a walk in that direction, she thought. There was probably a lot of interesting stuff heading toward the marshes.

She remembered when she was in middle school and they studied marsh ecology. Her teacher was from the low country of South Carolina too, and he'd been a wealth of information. Of course, being a kid, she hadn't been all that interested and remembered very little of what she was taught. It would've come in handy right about now.

Danielle turned toward the rocks and slowly

climbed up onto the stack. Surely there was an easier way to access this part of the beach. Older people would bust their heads left and right if they came this way. Maybe she'd missed another access point during her walk.

She finally made her way to the top, turned around and climbed down backward so she wouldn't fall flat on her face. When she felt her foot hit the sand below, she was relieved to have made it and was determined to find a better way back to the street. When she was done with her sightseeing, she'd look for another way home.

As she turned around, Danielle never expected to see what she saw. In fact, her eyes bugged out of her head so hard she feared she would have to chase them as they popped out and rolled toward the sea.

Laid out before her were over a dozen naked senior citizens. Some were lying on towels, taking in as much sunshine as a body can take. Others were standing in groups, chatting like they weren't letting everything God gave them hang out for the world to see.

She'd seen her share of body parts as a nurse, but she'd never happened upon a blatant display of things flipping and flopping about. She stood there, her hand on her heart, completely frozen. What did a fully clothed person do when she came across a naked village of retirees? Was it rude to be wearing clothes? Should she run? What if she tripped and fell face first into a mound of human flesh she couldn't identify?

Before she could decide on whether to run, cover her eyes or call the authorities, an older man came toward her. She didn't know exactly how old he was, but she had a flash in her mind of science class in elementary school when the teacher said you could find out the age of a tree by counting the rings inside the trunk. Could she count wrinkles and figure out this man's age? If so, she guessed one-hundred and two years old.

"You alright, honey?"

She stared at him. *No, sir, I'm not alright. You people are naked as jaybirds and something is wrong on this island.* She thought about it, but she couldn't say it.

"I… uh…" *Was it possible to swallow your tongue?* "I seem to have stumbled onto the wrong beach."

He laughed heartily, and things started to jiggle and shake. She quickly decided that looking at his ear was her best chance of avoiding that visual again. "This is Wisteria Island's nude beach, dear."

"Yes, I see that now," she said, avoiding his gaze like a dog who's gotten in trouble for digging through the trash.

"Care to join us?"

"No, thanks," she said, unsure of whether he was being sarcastic or serious.

"Want to get out of here as soon as possible?" he asked, obviously sensing her discomfort.

"Yes, please."

"Can you at least make eye contact with me, hon? I need to point you in the right direction."

She slowly looked back at him. "Sorry. I just wasn't expecting… this."

"It's not for everyone. Anyway, go right down there

between the pink and yellow houses. That'll take you back out to the main street."

"Thank you."

"I'm Peter, by the way," he said, reaching out his hand. She stifled a very immature laugh and shook his hand.

"Danielle. The new nurse."

"Oh, nice to meet you! I'll come see you soon. Got a rash I can't identify." She dared not look down to see where said rash was.

"Great. Looking forward to it."

Without further conversation, she quickly made her way back to the street, stopping long enough to take some deep breaths, wipe the sand off her feet and then laughed all the way home.

CHAPTER 4

*D*anielle was almost scared to walk into the diner after seeing so many of the residents in their birthday suits. She would never look at some of them the same way again. Thankfully, she barely knew anyone's name on the island anyway, but she could certainly point out people who had birthmarks in certain unmentionable areas.

"Good evening, Dani girl," Eddie said as she walked through the doorway. Tonight he was wearing a white suit, a black dress shirt with the collar up and white fake leather shoes.

"Hi, Eddie. What on earth are you wearing?"

He laughed loudly. "It's disco night! I'm John Travolta!"

"Sure you are," she muttered under her breath as she continued walking toward the food. She was hungry and just wanted to get this over with as soon as possible. She'd speak to a few people, gobble up her dinner and hide out in her cottage until tomorrow.

"Are you the new nurse?" a woman asked from behind her. She scooped the mashed potatoes onto her plate and turned around. "I am. My name is Danielle Wright."

The woman smiled, and Danielle finally felt a bit at ease. None of the residents, other than Eddie, had been overly welcoming so far, but this woman actually seemed nice.

"Oh good. I'm Gladys."

Danielle smiled. "Nice to meet you, Gladys."

"Want to sit with me?" she asked, pointing at her table. It seemed she was sitting alone, and Danielle felt bad for her since everyone else was sitting with other people. Maybe she felt as left out as Danielle did.

"Sure." She followed Gladys to her table and sat down. At first, there wasn't much conversation between them. Gladys munched on her dinner roll while Danielle scarfed down her meatloaf. It wasn't bad. In fact, she'd have to ask Bennett who did the cooking on Wisteria Island because it was quite good.

"Are you staying here?" Gladys finally asked.

"Pardon?"

"Well, everybody else leaves pretty dang quick. Are you staying?"

Danielle wasn't sure how to answer such a pointed question since she didn't know what she was going to do. She still had one foot on Wisteria Island and the other on that boat docked near her cottage.

"I certainly plan to."

Gladys giggled. "That means no."

Danielle cocked her head to the side. "Does it?"

"Nobody wants to stay here with us."

"I heard some nurses left. I'm sorry about that."

"We need somebody who will stick with us."

"I'm going to try my very best," Danielle said, not sure she really meant it.

"Have you seen the aliens yet?"

Danielle almost choked on her mashed potatoes. "Excuse me?"

"The aliens. They come at night-time. Usually on Tuesdays."

"I... um...."

"They land on the marsh and then walk the island looking for seashells. I think they study them."

"Okay..."

"Bob is the nice one. He brought me a moon rock, but I lost it."

"Gladys..."

"Oh, I see you've met dear Gladys here," Bennett suddenly said, seeming to come out of nowhere. He put his hands on Gladys's shoulders from behind and smiled at Danielle. "She's got quite an imagination, hasn't she? That's why she does so well in creative writing class."

Gladys smiled proudly. "I got an A on my essay."

"Creative writing class?"

"We believe keeping the residents busy and challenged helps to preserve cognitive function. Gladys takes part in just about everything we offer." He gave Danielle a look that indicated Gladys had some challenges with cognitive function.

"That's wonderful, Gladys. Keep up the excellent work!" Danielle said, trying to sound encouraging.

"I will. Well, I have to go to the bathroom now," Gladys said, suddenly standing up and walking off, leaving her plate on the table, practically untouched. Bennett pushed it to the side and sat down.

"Sorry about that. Gladys is very sweet, but she has some issues that can't be helped."

"Are you sure it can't be helped? I mean, has bloodwork been done? An MRI?"

"Well, no. We don't have an MRI machine here on the island."

"Bennett, surely you know people can leave the island and get testing done? Maybe Gladys needs that."

"Danielle, she's happy. Isn't that what matters? Not everyone can be fixed."

"But shouldn't we try?"

"She's seen her general practitioner, and he felt she has dementia, so we deal with it as best we can here. She's content, she has things to keep her busy and we love her like family. Her own family abandoned her."

Was that enough? Danielle wasn't sure. She felt like maybe Gladys would benefit from further testing. Were her hands going to be tied when treating her new patients?

"Can I ask you something?"

"Sure."

"Why didn't you warn me that there's a nude beach on this island?"

Bennett's face turned red as he stifled a laugh. "I

totally forgot about it. I just avoid that section of the beach. I'm so sorry. How bad was it?"

"Let's just say I'll never look at raisins or that guy named Peter the same way again!" She laughed so loudly that a few residents turned to look at her. It felt good to laugh. It'd been a long time since she'd done that.

"Again, I'm so sorry. It wasn't intentional, but it's nice to see you laugh."

There was an uncomfortable moment between them before Danielle coughed to break the tension. "Well, I'll know to avoid that area."

"They're only there between the hours of ten to four, so you're welcome to take night-time walks without seeing anything scary other than the occasional crab."

"Good to know," she said, taking the last bite of her food. "Well, I'd better get home. I've got a long day ahead of me tomorrow, and I need to get some sleep."

"Right. I understand. Hope the mattress works out well for you," he said, standing up.

"Thanks. See you later."

AFTER EDDIE DROPPED off her new mattress, Danielle laid back on it before even making the bed. She stared up at the ceiling, watching the fan blades go round and round until she almost gave herself vertigo.

This place didn't feel like home.

She was homesick. Not homesick enough to go

back, but homesick enough to want to cry. She wasn't a crier. She felt weak when she cried. She wanted to cry right now more than anything.

Instead, she decided to take a long, hot bath. As she walked into the bathroom, she heard her cell phone ringing on the kitchen counter where it was charging. She trotted into the kitchen and grabbed it on the third ring right before it would've gone to voicemail. She should've let it go to voicemail.

"Hello?"

"Danielle? Where on earth are you?" Her mother's voice was always unmistakable. It was what one might describe as shrill. Like a loud chainsaw, right outside your window on a Saturday morning.

"Hi, Mom."

"Why haven't you called me?"

"Because I'm getting settled into my new job."

"And where exactly is this new job?"

"South Carolina."

"What?" she shrieked. Danielle put it on speaker-phone to preserve her eardrums. "Why aren't you home?"

"You know why, Mom. I can't come back there."

"Danielle, you're overreacting to this whole situation."

"No, I'm not. Richard ruined my life, my career, my reputation. I'm a laughing stock."

"That's simply not true, Danielle. As usual, you're being overly dramatic."

Her mother had always said she was too dramatic, but Danielle knew that wasn't true. If anything, she was too practical, too pragmatic, and too devoid of emotions. She ran her life on autopilot, and that had worked until Richard blew everything out of the water.

"Thanks, Mom. I appreciate your support."

"Now, look, you know I love you. Men are men. Richard wasn't doing anything that every other man on this planet hasn't done. They're ruled by hormones and male genitalia."

"Don't make excuses for him!" She wanted to hang up, but it was her mother and she felt guilty doing that.

"It's not an excuse, dear, just an explanation. No man is ever completely trustworthy. I mean, look at your father…"

"And you divorced him. Yet I'm supposed to suck it up and go back to Richard? A little hypocritical, don't you think?"

"Your father and I had a lot more problems than him cheating with his hussy of a secretary."

"Maybe so, but Richard didn't just cheat, Mom. He was engaged to me and two other women in the same hospital! And he got one of them pregnant! Do you know how embarrassing it was to look so stupid? Me? The head of ICU nursing? A respected member of the medical community? Hearing people gossip about me all the time? About how stupid and clueless I was? Knowing that some of my so-called friends knew the entire time what he was doing?"

Her mother sighed. "I understand."

"No, you don't. You work in research. It's a totally different situation. I deal with people all day. You're staring at Petri dishes. Then the whole thing became local news and then a meme on social media? I just can't believe all of this happened so quickly."

"Danielle, either way, you need to go back. You had a great job and a wonderful life. You can get that back. You can find someone else."

"Mom, I'm not going back. I may not stay where I am, but I'm not going back there."

"Honey, you're not getting any younger. You're almost forty-years old. When are you going to settle down and start a family? You know the odds of you having a baby…"

"I need to go before I say something I'll regret."

"Danielle, please just think about it. Your job is still there waiting for you. Don't let Richard take that away from you. Go back with your head held high. You did nothing wrong. Please say you'll at least think about it."

"Fine. I'll think about it," she lied.

"Good."

She hung up, walked back to her bedroom and fell face-first onto her new mattress. A bath was too much work. Tonight she just needed to pass out, forget everything that had happened, and try to figure out how to blend into this weird little island.

BENNETT STOOD ON HIS DECK, staring out over the ocean. The light from the moon shone down and provided a dazzling show on the surface of the water, like little pieces of glass reflecting back at him. The beauty of his view was breathtaking each time he looked at it.

He sat down in his favorite chair and raised his glass of chardonnay. Most men drank beer, but he was a wine guy. His circle of friends had definitely swayed him in his choice of drink. Wine tastings used to be a common pastime for him, even though he hadn't drunk the stuff until he was well into his thirties.

He didn't like to think a lot about his past. It had been a tough upbringing since his mother raised him alone and had no money. She was a hard worker, but there were so many times that they'd had no food in the pantry and only an old box of baking soda in the refrigerator. He vividly remembered different chari-table organizations showing up at the door of their single-wide trailer with boxes of food, especially around the holidays. It was always an exciting time to rip open the boxes and find out what had been donated. His mother had always been frugal with what they would get, trying desperately to make it last.

Bennett had taken those experiences and tried to use his money to help others. He had two charities that gave food to the poor, and not just around the holiday season. People needed food all year round, and his organizations focused on that.

Although he'd adored his mother, he never wanted to be in that position again. With his financial wealth, he'd never be poor again. Mathematically, it was impossible unless he just suddenly gave all of his money away.

Still, he was poor in other areas of his life, mainly in

relationships. Finding a woman to share his life with had been difficult. Most were interested in his money and what he could buy them. When they found out he wasn't that stereotypical rich guy, they bolted. He was more interested in giving back to the world than buying fancy cars and partying on yachts.

What he'd learned about having money was that it didn't buy happiness. It bought opportunities. It bought stability. It bought freedom. It didn't buy happiness because happiness couldn't be bought. Happiness required trust and vulnerability. Happiness required jumping without a parachute. Bennett wasn't good at those things. Trust was not something that was hard-wired into him.

He had also learned that money just made people more of who they already were. So many of his wealthy friends just became greedier as they earned more money. Some people became more unhappy or more depressed. Money was like a spotlight that showed the true nature of the person who earned it.

He looked over at his phone sitting on the table next to him and thought for a moment about calling Danielle and asking how the mattress was working out. Realizing it sounded very inappropriate to ask an employee a question like that, he turned his phone off and finished his glass of wine.

Maybe the price of his wealth was being alone for the rest of his life. If that's what it cost him, it was a very high price.

~

DANIELLE HAD NEVER SLEPT SO WELL in her life. She'd snuggled into her new bed like someone who'd never had a bed. As she drifted off to sleep, she thought only briefly about her first day at work tomorrow. Would the patients like her? Would she like them? Would any of them show up nude?

She woke up once during the night to take a drink of water. Her cottage got awfully dry, especially since it was right on the water. She decided to buy a humidifier if she ever got back to the mainland. Maybe Amazon delivered there?

It didn't take her long to fall back asleep, and she was in a deep sleep when she heard the noise. A loud banging on her front door. Someone yelling. A man. A very gruff, deep-voiced man. Startled, she grabbed the baseball bat she'd brought with her for protection and headed toward the front door. Thankfully, she was wearing a full set of pajamas instead of her normal t-shirt only attire.

"Who's there?" she called from the other side of the door.

"Are you the nurse?" the man called, a hint of pain in his voice. She quickly unlocked the door and found a man standing there, doubled over. He was holding his right side and wincing.

"Here, let me help you," she said, gently taking his arm and helping him inside. She kicked the door shut behind her and helped him onto the small couch. He leaned back and groaned, a grimace on his face. "I'm Danielle. And you are?"

"Frank," he said, through painful breaths. "Frank

Cooper."

"Show me where the pain is, Frank."

He pointed to his upper right side, which made appendicitis unlikely. "What did you eat last?"

"Fried chicken."

"Frank, do you still have your gallbladder?"

"Yes," he said, his face contorting in pain.

"I believe you're having a gallbladder attack." She felt very under prepared, given that she had no medical tools at her new home. They were all sitting in her new office, which she hadn't visited yet. She looked down at her watch. Three-twenty in the morning.

"It hurts a lot," he said, turning slightly onto his left side to try to ease his pain.

"I know it does. I'm going to make a call, okay? Just stay right here." She ran to find her phone and quickly dialed Bennett's cell phone number. Thankfully, it was on his business card, and she'd programmed it into her phone for emergencies.

"Hello?" he said groggily.

"Bennett, it's Danielle."

"Danielle? Are you okay?" She thought it was a weird question, but she let it pass.

"Frank Cooper just showed up at my house, and I think he's having a gallbladder attack. He needs to be taken to the hospital."

"Oh wow. Okay. I'll call for transport and head to your place."

"Okay. Thanks." She hung up the phone and rushed back to Frank. He wasn't looking good, and she wondered if he might have pancreatitis instead of gallbladder issues. Without her normal imaging equipment, her hands were tied.

This wasn't what she was used to. In a hospital setting, she had access to blood testing, MRI and CT machines and the finest medical minds. On this island, she had a medical bag, a small office and a phone to call for paramedics. It made her feel limited. In that moment, she realized she was now much more of a small-town nurse than an experienced ICU professional.

A few minutes later, Bennett walked through the front door, his hair spiky and the look of sleep still in his eyes. "I called for help. They should be here within twenty minutes."

"Twenty minutes?" Frank yelled, groaning in pain as he clutched his right side.

"They're coming, Frank. Just hang on, okay?" Danielle said, rubbing his shoulder. Bennett motioned for her to come to the kitchen, away from Frank.

"Is he going to be okay?"

"I have no idea. I don't have any way to assess him on this island."

"He's eighty-one years old. I just hope they can get him to the hospital in time." She could tell Bennett was genuinely concerned.

"If it's gallbladder related, I think he'll be fine."

"Do you think that's what it is?"

"I'm really just guessing here, Bennett. But, yes, that's my best guess."

She was looking forward to getting into her office in a few hours and seeing exactly what tools she had for assessing her patients. If it wasn't adequate, she'd take up that fight with her new employer.

She continued working to make Frank as comfortable as possible, but gallbladder attacks were painful. There wasn't a lot she could do but hold his hand and tell him everything was going to be okay.

It seemed like forever before the paramedics finally arrived and transported Frank to the mainland. She assumed riding in a boat with a gallbladder attack wasn't exactly the most pleasant thing Frank had probably ever done.

"I hope he'll be all right. He really doesn't have any family. We're all he has," Bennett said as he watched the boat disappear out of sight. It was a dark night with very little moonlight.

"I'm sure they'll take good care of him." They turned and started walking back toward Danielle's cottage. "I'm exhausted. I have a big day tomorrow, so I'd better go try to get some sleep."

Bennett nodded. "You did a good job tonight, Danielle. I think you're going to fit in very well here."

She smiled and walked up the stairs to the porch. He might have had confidence in her, but she was questioning her decision to take the job on Wisteria Island more than ever. If her hands were tied when it came to taking care of the patients adequately, she didn't want the job.

CHAPTER 5

*T*he morning came early for Danielle. As she opened her eyes, the first glints of sunlight peaked through her blinds, assaulting her senses. It had been a long night, including when the hospital had called to let her know a status update on Frank.

Turned out she was right. It was his gallbladder, and he would get it removed today. They said that he could come home in a couple of days unless there were any complications. Of course, Danielle would need to help take care of him and make sure he wasn't overdoing it once he got back to the island.

She quickly got ready, downed a cup of coffee and a banana, and headed outside. It was a beautiful day, as most days were on the island, and she was looking forward to seeing her new office. Maybe she would be pleasantly surprised, although that hadn't been her experience so far on the island.

"Hey there!" Gladys said, waving as she walked by.

She had a little dog on a leash, dressed up in a pink tutu.

"Good morning, Gladys. How are you today?"

Gladys stopped and shrugged her shoulders. "It's always a good day if I wake up on this side of the ground."

Danielle laughed. "I guess that's one way to look at it. Well, I had better be going. First day at work."

She smiled. "Can I give you a piece of advice?"

"Of course."

"Don't let these old fogeys get you down!" With that, she continued walking her little dog, humming a song loudly to herself as she went.

Danielle wasn't sure exactly what was going on in Gladys' brain, but maybe she was just happier than everybody else. Maybe they were the ones with the problem, and Gladys was doing just fine.

As she turned left down the main street where most of the businesses were, she found her office tucked between the coffee shop and the salon. She pulled the key that Bennett had given her out of her pocket and unlocked the door. Thankfully, nobody was there yet, so she'd have a bit of time to look around.

Naomi had texted her and let her know that the schedule was pretty full, starting around eight AM. That would give her about thirty minutes to get her bearings before the first patient arrived.

When she walked in, she was pretty surprised to find such a spacious office. There was a nice, large waiting room with a flat screen TV on the wall. The big picture window overlooked the street, and her office was across from the sandwich shop so she could see people milling about for the day.

Beyond the waiting room was the door to the back, where she would be working. She opened it and found three exam rooms and a central area with a large table top for her to work. There was already a laptop sitting there, along with tongue depressors, cotton balls, and gauze pads.

She looked around for an x-ray machine but found none. That would be the first thing on her list to bug Bennett about. An x-ray machine was the very bare minimum that a nurse would need to care for an island full of elderly people. What if somebody broke a hip?

Thankfully, she found equipment to run blood-work. She would definitely need that. Of course, there was no CT or MRI machine, and she didn't like her chances of ever getting that kind of thing. If she could get the x-ray machine and run bloodwork, she might have a chance of really being able to help people.

A part of what she liked to do in her spare time was study natural health remedies. Of course, working in the ICU didn't lend itself well to that sort of thing, so she was looking forward to being able to branch out a bit. Still, she was unsure about this job. Did she really want to give up the big, prestigious career she'd built and opt instead to take care of an island full of rapidly aging people? Today would be an interesting adventure.

Just as she was sanitizing each of the rooms, she heard the front door open. Evidently, her first patient of the day had arrived.

When she walked out into the waiting room, it surprised her to see Morty standing there. He didn't look nearly as happy as he had when she met him at dinner the other night. Dressed in a simple golf shirt and tan slacks, he wasn't wearing his flamboyant attire.

"Hi, Morty. I didn't expect to see you here this morning."

"Well, dear, it's been a rough day so far. I believe my blood pressure is acting up."

"Well, that's not good. Come on back and I'll check it."

Morty followed her to the back and sat down in a little chair next to the blood pressure machine. She put it around his small arm and pressed the button. Many people liked to take blood pressure manually, but she was pretty happy relying on the machine to do it.

"Oh, goodness, your blood pressure is a bit high. Do you take a beta blocker or a calcium channel blocker?"

He stared at her, his eyes wide. "I don't take any medications."

"You don't? None?"

"No, ma'am. I made it to the ripe old age of sixty-seven years old without taking medications. I don't plan to start now!"

"Well, this blood pressure is pretty high. In your age bracket, that makes it very dangerous. I suggest we get you on a prescription of beta blockers to help..."

He put up his little hand, which was adorned with several gaudy rings. "Honey, I'm not taking any pills."

"Can I ask you why?"

Morty smiled. "I'm one of those hippie dippy

granola eating natural health kind of people. You should've seen me back in the sixties. I was a sight to behold," he said, smiling.

"But you understand that having high blood pressure is very dangerous. You could have a stroke or heart attack."

"Darling, anything could happen to any of us. I hoped that you could help me figure out some holistic things to do to help my blood pressure."

She smiled and squeezed his shoulder before taking off the blood pressure cuff. "That's not really my forte. I am much more of a Western medicine-based nurse, although I have been doing some studying about juicing. I don't know a whole lot about natural blood pressure reduction."

"Well, we can all change, can't we?"

"Morty, it sounds like you really need to see a nutritionist or something along those lines."

"You're a nurse. You're supposed to help us," he said, a more stern look on his face.

"I'm trying to help you. My advice is to take a beta blocker."

He groaned under his breath. "This is why other nurses don't last here. You must be the most inflexible people God ever made. The people of this island came here because they're different. We want to live long, healthy lives. We don't want to be put on a bunch of pills and treated like we don't matter." He turned and started walking toward the door.

"Morty! I didn't mean to offend you. It's just that I

think you should be on medication for your blood pressure..."

He turned around. "If you're going to stay here, you have to adjust to the island. The people of this island will not adjust to you," he said, staring at her for a moment longer before turning and walking out the door.

Danielle was stunned. He seemed so happy-go-lucky, so laid-back. What on earth had caused him to get so riled up that quickly? Feeling a little shellshocked, she was glad that she had a few minutes before her next patient was due to arrive. If everybody acted like this, she might need blood pressure medicine by the end of the day.

BENNETT WONDERED how Danielle was getting on with her patients. He was afraid to stop by and ask for fear that she might actually tell him.

He knew today was pivotal. Every other nurse had left almost right after their first day. Very few of them had stayed much longer. The residents of the island could be challenging, to say the least. Each one of them had their own distinct personality, and they all depended on the nurse.

He thought many times about hiring more than one nurse or bringing on a doctor. It'd been stressful enough just trying to keep a nurse on the island, much less a staff of medical professionals.

Still, he knew that the people who lived on the

island were different. They were there for that very reason. Most of their families had decided they didn't want to be bothered with them. Or they felt like they didn't fit in and wanted to go somewhere they would be accepted.

Nobody on the island was there accidentally.

Bennett remembered going on a cruise one time in December. Not having a lot of family, he had decided to get away for the holidays. He was sitting at a table full of people that seemed absolutely crazy. They had assigned him to sit with these people at dinner time, and he wished he could've ordered room service for every meal.

When he was talking to one worker on the ship, she explained that the craziest people went on cruises in December because their own family didn't want them home for the holidays. Bennett thought she was joking, but when he started running the island he realized that sometimes families really do cast off members that don't fit in.

But he loved all the residents of the island, the difficult ones and the easy ones. He accepted them all. He still had hope that Danielle could do the same.

Deciding that he couldn't take the temptation any longer, he went to grab a sandwich for lunch and see if he could just peek through the window of her office to make sure she wasn't preparing to jump off the roof of the building or something.

After getting his sandwich, he walked back out onto the sidewalk and noticed Danielle coming out of her office door, locking it behind her. They stared at each other from across the street for a moment.

"Hey!" he said, raising his hand up and smiling. She didn't smile back. Instead, she sauntered across the street and stood in front of him, her arms crossed.

"Why didn't you tell me?"

"Tell you what?" he said, playing innocent.

"Bennett, the residents of this island are some of the most difficult people I've ever dealt with. I started the day with Morty, who got mad because I wanted to put him on medication for his blood pressure. I had one woman who yelled at me because her knee hurts and I can't do anything about it. Another man came to talk to me about a rash in a place I won't mention. Look, I've dealt with all kinds of patients in my career, but usually they actually want my help. They don't fight me on every little thing."

"Please don't tell me any more. I don't want to know." He hung his head. "Are you leaving?"

"I don't know."

Bennett sighed. "Please don't leave. You have to earn their trust. They'll settle down once you do."

"What if I don't want to?"

"What do I need to do to make this easier for you?"

"Well, for one thing, I need an x-ray machine. It's very unsafe not to have one here."

"Fine. I will get an x-ray machine."

"And I need the authority to take some additional training on some holistic healing methods. Herbs, vitamins, things like that."

"Done. Whatever you need."

"And I need you to buy me a sandwich because I left my purse at the office."

He laughed. "You don't need money here. Just go in there and order a sandwich."

"This is the strangest place I've ever been in my life," she said, as she walked past him and into the sandwich shop.

DANIELLE SAT down for what seemed like the first time that day. She put her feet up on a nearby stool, leaned her head back, and sighed. She never expected her plate to be so full of patients, especially on her first day of working as the island nurse. Patient after patient saw her, many saying that they had waited weeks to get medical care because all the nurses kept leaving.

Some residents were nice to her, like Mr. Jefferson, whom she'd met that day. He never stopped smiling and making jokes. He reminded her a lot of a patient she once had in the ICU. His name was Philip, and he was almost ninety-years old when she met him. For weeks, he was in a coma, but one day he just opened his eyes like nothing happened. He immediately started making jokes until they wheeled him out to a rehab facility one day. She'd missed his positive attitude so much after he was gone, and she often wondered how he was doing.

There were other residents who weren't so welcoming. Many were suspicious of her for reasons she didn't understand. Wisteria Island felt a bit like a commune or some kind of secret club that she had to earn membership into, but she wasn't sure how. She wasn't even sure she wanted to stay there.

"Hello?"

She slowly stood up and walked out into the waiting area. There she found a tiny older woman. She looked like a miniature human being, like Danielle could pick her up and put her in the pocket of her medical jacket.

"Hi. I'm Danielle Wright, the new nurse. And you are?"

"Emmy Lou," the woman said, her voice so tiny and squeaky. She was adorable with her little red hat, white blouse with lace neckline and cuffs and her red dress pants all ironed with the seam down the front. "Dressed to the nines" is what her grandmother would've called it.

"Well, it's nice to meet you, Emmy Lou. What can I do for you today?"

She smiled. "It's not what you can do for me, sweetie. It's what I can do for you."

"Pardon?"

"I brought you something." She reached into the tote bag she was holding and pulled out a small, round metal canister. It was definitely an older canister, like something you'd find at an antique store. "Here you go."

Danielle took the canister and smiled. She popped open the top to find a stack of what looked to be oatmeal raisin cookies. Thankfully, she was one of those people who loved them. In her experience, people either loved or hated oatmeal raisin cookies. They weren't widely accepted like chocolate chip cookies. They were the outsiders of the cookie world. Rebels.

"Thank you. They look amazing!"

"They're my mother's recipe."

"You're the first person to bring me a gift, so thank you."

Emmy Lou sighed. "I'm sorry not everyone here is so welcoming. Mind if I sit?"

"Oh, of course. Please," she said, pointing to the small row of chairs against the wall. She joined Emmy Lou, happy to be off of her feet for a while longer.

"I'm ninety-six years old."

Danielle was shocked. "You are? Wow! You don't look…"

"That old?" she said, giggling.

"I didn't mean it that way…"

Emmy Lou patted her knee. "No worries, my dear. I am old, and that's a good thing. God has allowed me to live a long, happy life, although I've had my share of strife. Lost my husband when I was thirty years old and never remarried. Never had kids."

"I'm sorry for your loss."

She smiled. "I still miss him, you know. Even all these years later. They say grief gets better with time, but that's not really true. It just changes and morphs, much like the water hitting a rock for years and years. The rock still stays there, but it's ever changing. It never looks quite the same."

"How's your health?"

"Good, I suppose. I have creaky old bones, and I can't work in my garden anymore, but I think I'm doing pretty good for an old lady. I enjoy going to church, reading a bit and watching my stories on TV."

"Your stories?"

She laughed. "I think you young folks call them soap operas."

"Ah, I see. So, what did you want to chat about today?"

"I just wanted to welcome you here and say that I do hope you'll stay with us. So many people need you here, even if they won't admit it."

"Why is that, Emmy Lou? Why are some people so unwelcoming?"

She sighed. "Lots of reasons, I guess. We keep getting nurses, and then they leave because they can't handle the needs of our residents. There are some quirky people here, you know. People whose own families don't want them around. I don't have a family, so this was a godsend to me. Bennett is like the grandson I never had."

"I'm glad you had this option. You have no family at all?"

"Well, I've got some great-nieces and great-nephews, but they have busy lives, you see."

That made Danielle sad, but not surprised. People often forgot about the older members of their families when it came time to take care of them. So many ended up in nursing homes or assisted living with no visitors. It was sad, and it angered her. She was always surprised how many people left their loved ones in the hospital, only occasionally checking in by phone.

"So you enjoy living here then?"

"Oh, I love it. This is a fun place to live. You'll see."

"I hope so."

"I have a feeling that maybe you need this place too, Danielle."

"Why do you say that?"

"Being almost a century old, you just pick up on things. I feel like you came here for a reason, and this island will heal you."

It was a comforting thought, but not one Danielle was buying into at the moment. The island would heal her?

"Well, thank you for the cookies."

Emmy Lou stood up slowly and put her tote bag over her shoulder. "It was very nice to meet you, but I've got a ladies' church social to get to now."

"It was nice to meet you too."

As she watched Emmy Lou slowly toddle down the sidewalk, she bit into one of the cookies. As expected, they tasted like heaven.

CHAPTER 6

*D*anielle saw patient after patient during her first week on the island, getting to know each one as she went. Some were quite nice, like Emmy Lou. Others were downright mean, but she maintained her professionalism as best she could. Still, she missed her old life. Her simple life. Her familiar life.

She missed her friends at the hospital, at least the ones she had left. The ones who hadn't gossiped about her or relished in her downfall. The ones who hadn't taken part in the demise of her career. They were few and far between.

She missed her apartment and the view of the city. She missed her neighbor's dog, Buddy, who would scratch at her door every morning, wanting a bite of the banana she put in her oatmeal. She even missed the commute to the hospital. Each morning, she'd stop at her favorite coffee shop, where they knew her well, and get her caramel latte with extra whipped cream.

She missed the feeling of familiarity. The feeling of

being included. The feeling of being needed in a way that allowed her to play the hero. The grief and loss were almost overwhelming to her, taking her breath away when she thought too hard about it all.

Today was her day off, at least in theory. As the main medical professional on the island, she was always on call, but today was her catch-up day. She'd do her laundry and do some grocery shopping at the very least.

She pulled the sheets off her bed and tossed them into the washing machine, the heavy door shutting with a loud thud. Just as she was about to turn the dial, her phone rang in the pocket of her baggy warm-up pants.

"Hello?" she said, without even looking at the caller ID. She turned the dial on the washing machine and quickly exited the laundry room, shutting the door behind her.

"Danielle? It's me, Carla."

"Carla? How are you?" She hadn't expected to hear from one of her previous work friends, but it was nice to hear a familiar voice that wasn't her mother's.

"Are you okay? Where are you? Everybody is worried."

Danielle laughed under her breath. "Really? Everybody wasn't worried about me while my fiancé was sleeping around and getting engaged to every woman he saw."

Carla sighed. "I told you I didn't know, Danielle. Not until right before you found out."

"You knew for two entire weeks, Carla. We were friends, or at least I thought so."

"I didn't know what to do! Richard is my friend too…"

"*Is*? He *is* your friend? Seriously? How could you stay friends with him after what he did to me?"

"I've known Richard for over ten years. We work together every day. Was I supposed to just stop speaking to him?"

Danielle knew this was going nowhere good. "Carla, we've been over this a million times, and I don't want to rehash it. Why are you calling me?"

"We've been worried about you, like I said."

"We?"

"The nursing staff, Dr. Milner, Eloise in the cafeteria and… Richard."

She felt anger welling up inside of her. "What?"

"Richard is devastated by all of this, Danielle. He feels terrible."

"He should feel terrible. I worked for fifteen years to get to that position and earn the respect that I had. He destroyed that!" She walked out onto the back deck and sat down in a chair, her eyes fixed on the ocean waves. She had to do something to keep herself calm.

"Would you consider coming back?"

Danielle laughed loudly. "You can't be serious!"

"Richard says he needs you here. The ICU doesn't run the same without you. Also, he broke off his engagements."

"So what? He still did what he did, and he has a baby on the way!"

"He said he wants DNA testing…"

"Oh my gosh, Carla! Why are you making this call for him?"

She sighed. "I miss you. I need you back here."

"Well, I'm not coming back. Ever."

"Danielle, please reconsider. You may never get an opportunity like this again. Running the ICU was your dream job. Don't let all of this ruin that for you. Besides, they're going to be filling your job if you don't come back soon. I heard LaRusse talking about it this morning," she said, lowering her voice at the end.

LaRusse was the Human Resources Director at the hospital, and Danielle knew he was quick about filling vacant positions. She couldn't blame him, given the fact that they were one of the largest hospitals in the region and needed a strong ICU.

For some reason, the thought of her old job getting filled gave her a bit of anxiety she hadn't expected. Maybe deep down she'd thought that no one could fill her shoes or that they'd spend months looking for a replacement. A part of her hadn't let it go.

"I would never work with Richard again."

"Between you and me, he's being investigated by human resources right now. I don't know how much longer he'll keep his job."

Danielle closed her eyes and took a deep breath before blowing it out. "Listen, it was good to hear from you, but I have to go," she said, ready to press end.

"Wait! Will you just think about it? I know LaRusse has interviews starting Wednesday. Give it through the weekend and let me know, okay?"

"Carla, it's over. I'm sorry. I just can't come back there."

There was a long moment of silence between them. "I really hate that this is how it worked out. Our patients were better because you were here."

"I'm sure LaRusse will find someone great. Now, I really have to go, okay?"

"Okay. Bye, Danielle."

"Bye," she said, ending the call before Carla could hear her choke up. She truly hated this whole situation.

Danielle stared out into the ocean. It really was beautiful on Wisteria Island. It felt like she'd stepped back in time with the quaint streets and quiet lifestyle. Although wonderful for some people, she often found herself feeling antsy and lonely.

Going from working in such a fast-paced environment to Wisteria Island was jarring. She didn't know if she'd make it there long-term. Maybe she'd look for another position at a big hospital. Maybe she'd try Nashville or Tampa or the Caribbean or another country. As far away from Richard as possible was her motto.

Then there was the stubborn part of her that hated that she'd let him take her favorite job away from her. Climbing up the ranks hadn't been easy. He was still there, having his career and prestige, while she was dealing with an island of misfit old people who waffled between hating her and needing her. How had this happened? He'd made the mistakes, and she'd suffered the consequences. How was that even fair?

Had she been too quick to leave? Had her pride

caused her to run away? She was the victim in all of it, yet she'd lost the most.

As she felt the hot tears stinging her face, she leaned her head back and closed her eyes, allowing the ocean breeze to dry her face. Just as fast as it dried, she covered it in tears again. This was the most she'd cried since the day she found out what Richard had done. Maybe this was her moment of catharsis. Maybe there was hope she could start again.

BENNETT STARED out over the water, paying special attention to a seagull that was constantly dive bombing into the water. For a moment, he felt kind of guilty that he was a human and able to order the delectable tuna melt that was in front of him, while the poor bird had to exert so much energy just to get lunch. Life wasn't always fair.

"Are you going to eat that or stare at that blasted bird all day?" Morty was sitting across from him, gorging himself on a large grilled chicken salad. Bennett liked to have lunch with the residents when he could, and Morty was among his favorite dates. He loved eating at the open-air cafe overlooking the beach. There was nothing better than good food and a beautiful view of the ocean.

"Don't you think it's unfair that birds have to work so hard to get their food while we just order from a menu?" Bennett asked, finally taking a bite of his food. Morty stared at him.

"Have you been day-drinking?"

Bennett laughed. "No. Just pondering life's imponderables, I guess."

Morty rolled his eyes. "I learned a long time ago that one shouldn't have such deep thoughts." He leaned in and whispered, "It'll give you digestive issues, if you know what I mean."

"Okay, let's change the subject," Bennett said, worried that he wouldn't have an appetite before long.

"Fine. Then let's talk about that nurse you hired. What's her deal?"

"What do you mean?"

"Well, she tried to push pills on me, for one thing."

"I'm sure that's not true, Morty."

He slapped his hand lightly on the table for effect. "It most certainly is true! But, besides that, she seems to hate it here. Her face is shaped into a permanent frown."

"I think she had something happen in her life before she came here."

Morty leaned across the table, a grin on his face. "Like what? You think maybe she's a fugitive or something?"

"No, I don't," Bennett said. "But you'd be a great gossip columnist."

"So what is it then?"

Bennett chuckled. "I don't know, and it's none of our business, anyway. Don't you dare press her about it either."

Morty took another bite of his food, crunching down on the crisp lettuce. Bennett felt like he was eating lunch with a very hungry rabbit. "You have a little crush, don't you?"

"Excuse me?"

Morty laughed and clapped his hands together several times. "I can always tell! You like her!"

"I do not like her, at least not like that. She's my employee."

"The heart wants what it wants," Morty said, making the words into a song.

"What would you know about that, anyway?"

He smiled. "I've experienced a lot of love in my life, actually. But we're talking about you. Why don't you make a play for her? She's cute, even if she made me mad."

Bennett chuckled. "Eat your salad. I have a video meeting in an hour."

"Oh poo! You're no fun."

DANIELLE STRETCHED her arms high above her head and let out the groan that she had been holding in all morning. Seeing patients this way was a lot more tiring than she thought it would be. ICU life had been much more fast-paced, but taking time to sit and listen to each of her patients, for sometimes a half an hour or more, was proving to be exhausting.

She'd been at it since eight o'clock this morning, only taking time for a quick snack around eleven when she'd scarfed down an apple and string cheese. Each of her patients had been difficult, as usual.

One woman had gout and argued with her about taking medication. Another woman couldn't understand why she needed to stop her rollerskating lessons given that she had pretty severe osteoporosis.

There was just something about the people on this island that made Danielle want to pull her hair out by the roots. Each one of them had their own quirky nature, almost like Bennett had somehow pulled together the most stubborn old people he could find across the globe.

She had one more patient before lunch, and then she was going to take a leisurely stroll down to the beach and eat the chicken salad croissant she'd picked up from the sandwich shop across the street. She had found that the food on Wisteria Island was actually very good.

"Hello?" she heard an older man call from the waiting room. The door had just chimed, so she knew he hadn't been waiting more than maybe three seconds before he started calling out. That was never a good sign. Impatient patients were the worst.

"Just a moment. I'm coming," Danielle said, taking a deep breath and blowing it out before she rounded the corner. She'd been doing a lot more breathing techniques and meditation lately just trying to keep her wits about her.

It was strange because she should've been a lot more stressed out working at a hospital, but that felt more natural to her than working individually with patients who only wanted to argue with her. Plus, there was the fact that when she was at the hospital, she worked with patients from all age ranges. On Wisteria Island, she wondered just how much good she could possibly do in a population of older people. How could she keep them healthier? How could she keep them alive longer? These were questions she never really had to ask herself when she was dealing with a thirty-year-old in the ICU after a biking accident. Her job was to keep them alive and send them home, of course, but then her job was over. Wisteria Island felt like a long-term responsibility that she wasn't sure she was cut out for even now.

As she rounded the corner, she saw an older gentleman standing there, his arms crossed. He was tall and thin with perfectly styled gray hair and completely clean shaven. If she hadn't known better, she would've thought he was a Wall Street stockbroker or perhaps an attorney.

"I assume you're the new nurse?" he said, his tone short and snippy.

"That's me. I'm Danielle. And you are?"

"Theodore Donovan."

He said it with such authority, like she should've been impressed. She searched her brain to think whether she'd ever heard his name before.

"It's nice to meet you, Theodore."

He glared at her. "You know, my mother taught me to call my elders Mr. or Mrs. I guess today's generation is a little different."

"I'm happy to call you Mr. Donovan, if that makes you feel more comfortable," she said with a forced smile. "Why don't you follow me to the exam room?"

Without waiting for an answer, she turned and walked through the doorway, listening to the click of his expensive dress shoes on the floor as they walked.

She flipped the light on in room three and waited for him inside. He walked in, making no eye contact, and sat down in a chair rather than on the table. She sat on her wheeled stool and looked at him.

"So, what can I help you with, Mr. Donovan?"

"My wife sent me here. I've been having some issues in a particular area."

"Care to elaborate on what area that is?"

He stared at her. She could tell he was growing irritated already, but she had no idea why.

"Do I really have to go into detail?"

"I'm afraid so. I don't really know what you're talking about."

He let out a loud sigh and leaned in closer. "The flagpole isn't going up anymore, if you get my drift."

Suddenly, Danielle was faced with something she hadn't been faced with in her entire career. Nobody talked about erectile dysfunction in the ICU. It was typically the last thing on anyone's mind. Here sat this very frustrated and irritated man, staring at her as she made the mental connection between a flagpole and a male body part.

"Oh. I'm sorry. That took me a minute to understand," she said, stumbling over her words as she looked down at her clipboard. At the hospital, she would've been using an electronic tablet, but Wisteria Island wasn't exactly a mecca of technology.

"Look, I don't want anybody on this island knowing

I've got this issue. I just want you to give me some of those pills I see on the TV late at night so I can move on with my life. It's almost our sixtieth wedding anniversary, and I'm tired of hearing my wife nag me about it."

"Mr. Donovan, I can't just write you a prescription for pills. First of all, I'm a nurse. So I would have to clear it with the doctor when he comes to the island. Second of all, I think you need to be evaluated."

He tilted his head to the side. "Evaluated? Exactly how do they evaluate you for something like that?"

"Well, it might be a good idea for you to see a urologist…"

"Negative. Nobody is poking around down there except for my wife."

Danielle struggled not to laugh. "I'm more concerned that you see a cardiologist. Have you seen one before?"

"My heart is fine. I saw one probably ten years ago, and this ticker works just great. Besides, what does that have to do with… well, you know."

"The blood vessels in the male genitalia region are some of the tiniest in the body. When men have issues down there, it's often the first sign of hardening of the arteries in the heart and other parts of the body."

He sat there quietly for a moment. "Nobody has ever told me that before."

"Well, it's true, and I would really feel better about getting you on medication if we got your heart checked out first. I just want to make sure there's nothing going on there that we are ignoring."

She saw his face change slightly, almost a look of gratitude washing across it. "You seem pretty smart."

"Thank you."

"So how do I go see this heart doctor?"

"I can give you a referral to someone on the mainland. I'm not sure how long it will take you to get an appointment, so why don't I try to make a call today and I'll get back to you. Sound good?"

He nodded his head before standing up. "Thanks."

She followed him back up front. "I'll call you a little later today."

He reached for the door, but then turned around. "You know, we've had a lot of nurses here in the last couple of years. I've given them all a run for their money, but I think you might be the best one we've had."

Danielle smiled. "Well, I think that might be a high praise coming from you, Mr. Donovan."

He chuckled under his breath and nodded. "You can call me Ted."

She laughed as she watched him walk down the sidewalk toward his house. Why did everybody give her such a hard time? Bennett hadn't been kidding when he said she'd have to prove herself to everybody on that island.

DANIELLE WAS glad that her workday was done. She was tired, hungry and ready to pile into her bed, watch a pointless television show and eat ice cream until her stomach hurt. That had become her new normal, and it wasn't something she ever expected. If her yoga pants started getting tight, she'd have to make different nutritional decisions.

She locked the door to her office and stepped out onto the sidewalk. It was another beautiful day on Wisteria Island; the blue sky didn't have a cloud in it.

"How was your day?" Bennett always seemed to be hiding around the corner from wherever she was.

"I'm not sure of the word I would use to describe it, but I'm going to say it was taxing."

He frowned. "I had hoped that today would be easier for you. Who did you see?"

"Too many to count. But I think it was Mr. Theodore Donovan that really threw me for a loop."

"Good old Ted. He likes to really test out the nurses. He used to be a trial attorney back in his younger days. I heard he's having some issues that might have been hard to discuss?"

"Patient confidentiality, Bennett."

She started walking towards her house, the whole time thinking that she needed to get an electric bike or a golf cart of her own. After a long day, it was exhausting to walk back to the cottage.

Bennett walked alongside her, although she really wanted him to leave her alone so she could get home as quickly as possible. She enjoyed his company, and he wasn't bad to look at, but right now she was focused on just doing her job, getting a paycheck and trying to figure out her next move.

"Have you made any decisions about staying?"

She looked over at him. "No, I haven't. I don't know when I will. I didn't sign a contract for a particular period of time."

"I know. I'm not trying to pressure you. You've already stayed longer than ninety percent of the other nurses, so I was hoping it was good news."

"It's just a different type of lifestyle than I'm used to. I work with all different age ranges at the hospital, and here I'm not sure how much good I can do. I mean I can only prolong people's lives to a certain extent, and that's only if they want to do the work."

"I'm not sure it's about prolonging anybody's life. It's just about making sure these people have good medical care and the support of somebody who listens to them. Many of them come to you because they don't have anyone else to talk to."

"They seem to talk to you just fine," she said with a laugh.

"Well, I've always been the patient kind. My mom used to say that I was too patient."

"I guess there are things that are worse than being too patient," she said, slowing down a bit so he could catch up.

"I think you're doing a great job. I've heard some talk on the island, and people are getting comfortable with you."

"They sure don't show it when they come for a visit," she said, smiling.

"Listen, these people appreciate you a lot more than you realize. You just have to know they all have interesting personalities."

Danielle stopped and sat down on one of the benches dotting the sidewalk. "Interesting is one way to describe it."

He sat down beside her. "I think it will help you to know more about them when you come to the ice cream social."

She craned her neck and looked at him. "Ice cream social? What is that?"

"Naomi didn't give you the information? I'll have to talk to her about that. The ice cream social is next week on Wednesday. It's family visit day."

"Wait. Family is coming?"

"Yes, but don't worry. There's not much you have to do. All the medical testing to make sure we're only bringing healthy people onto the island is done on the mainland. The doctor has a staff of people who handle that."

"How long will they be here?"

"They typically stay from Wednesday until Saturday. That gives everybody plenty of time to spend with their loved ones, and they get to have some fun. The beaches get a lot more crowded, so I will warn you about that."

"So I'm going to get to meet the family members of these people?"

"Some of them. There are those who can't make it, and there are some who don't have any family members. It can be a little sad for those people."

"I bet. Maybe you should consider bringing in a counselor who can work with some of the residents when they are struggling with feelings of abandonment."

Bennett smiled. "See? You're starting to care about these people."

"I care about all people. Don't read too much into it."

He shrugged his shoulders just as her phone started ringing. "You take that in private. See you at dinner tonight?"

Dinner. She got really tired of having to go to dinner every single night, but it was part of her job description. She nodded and waved as he walked down the sidewalk. Pulling her phone out of her pocket, she pressed answer before even looking down to see who it was.

"Hello?"

"Danielle? It's your mother."

Dang, she should have looked at the caller ID.

"Hi, Mom. What can I do for you?"

"Well, I've got the most exciting news!"

"And what is that?"

"They have fired Richard from the hospital. That means you can go back now!"

She sat there for a moment, her stomach churning just hearing his name. A part of her was happy that he had finally gotten fired. Long-awaited justice was better than no justice at all.

"Danielle? Are you still there?"

"Yes. I'm still here."

She knew her mother was asking if she was still on

the other end of the phone, but she was looking around at Wisteria Island and noting that she was still *there*.

"So? Do you want me to call the hospital and let them know that you're coming back?"

"No! Why on earth would I want my mother to call the hospital about my previous job when I'm a grown woman?"

"Fine. You can call them. I'm sure they'll be delighted to hear that you're coming back."

She sat there for a moment and noticed Gladys toddling down the sidewalk with her little white dog. Always smiling and happy, Gladys waved at her and then turned down a side street, probably heading towards the beauty salon.

"Danielle?"

"I'm not calling them."

"What?"

"Look, I have a job. I took this job in good faith, and I am going to give it my best."

"Danielle, you can't be serious. You have a fantastic education and all of this work experience. You cannot be serious that you're going to stay on a little island of old people. How are you ever going to find a husband?"

"What if I don't need a husband? What if that's not the first thing on my mind? What if I just want to be happy?"

Her mother laughed under her breath. "Happiness is overrated, dear."

"Mom, I have to go. I need to take a shower before I go eat dinner with my residents."

"Danielle, don't make a big mistake. Go take back what's yours!"

"We'll talk later, Mom." Of course. Next time she planned to pay much closer attention to her caller ID before she answered the phone.

anielle stood outside with the rest of the staff, wearing the purple Wisteria Island T-shirt they had all been given. It was important for the family members to know who was staff and who was a resident, although most of the residents outpaced her by at least thirty or forty years.

It was a hotter than a typical day, the wind not whipping around as it normally did, so she was feeling the effects of the heat as she waited for the ferry to pull up. Bennett had rented a ferry instead of using the smaller boat just because of the sheer number of people coming to the island for a visit.

Eddie said that he used a bigger boat every year so that they could pick up all the family members in one trip rather than going back-and-forth all day long. Eager residents stood beside the staff members, anxiously awaiting the arrival of their family members.

Danielle assumed it had to be quite difficult for them to only see their family members a couple of times a year, although some of them used video chats frequently. Still, she guessed that there would be many joyous reunions happening in front of her in the next few minutes.

"Excited?" Bennett asked as he walked up beside her.

"Breathless with anticipation," she said dryly, before laughing. "Does this usually go pretty well?"

He shrugged his shoulders. "Not always. Some of these people don't really want to visit, but they feel guilty. Other residents don't get any visitors at all. I try to give them more attention during this time."

She nodded her head. "I'll do the same. It always makes me so mad when families dump their parents or grandparents somewhere and don't come back. It's the same way I feel when somebody drops their dog off at the shelter just because they don't want to be bothered with them anymore."

"Yeah, it's very sad."

A few moments later, the ferry arrived at the small dock. Staff members who were familiar with the process walked toward it and started helping people off one by one.

As anticipated, Danielle watched some people rejoice in their reunion, hugging and laughing. Others were much quieter in their approach to their loved one, simply walking up and saying hello with little contact. And then there were the residents who stood there, hoping someone was coming, and then no one appeared.

This seemed to be the case for Morty. Bennett had

worried about that and had relayed those fears to Danielle a couple of days before. Morty had family, but they often forgot about him and rarely video chatted. Morty always got his hopes up and stood by the dock on the slight chance that someone would show.

"Are you okay, Morty?" Danielle asked as she walked up behind him and put her hand on his shoulder. They had mended fences from the last time he was mad at her, and she had learned how to deal with his quirky personality. In fact, he was one of her favorites on the island, although she'd never tell anyone that.

He smiled sadly and looked up at her. "I don't know why I ever think my family might change. They've never been accepting of me. They are all quite prim and proper, and I'm a little colorful for their taste."

"Well, I think you're amazing!"

He cocked his head to the side. "You do?"

"Of course! Your fashion sense alone is something to behold. Plus, you're one of the funniest people I've ever met. So, if your family can't see that, it's really their loss."

He reached over and squeezed both of her hands. "Thank you for that. I really do appreciate it. I think I'm going to head home and take a nice long bubble bath. I'll see you at the ice cream social. I never miss a chance to have a nice ice cream cone!"

She nodded and smiled as she watched him walk away, sure that he was probably going to have himself a good cry in that bubble bath. She did that often. There was just something about being alone in a big tub of hot water that gave her the permission to let all of her emotions out.

"I see they didn't show up again," Bennett said, gritting his teeth.

"Yeah, and he was pretty upset. Morty is such an amazing guy. I don't understand why his family disowned him like that."

"People just don't want to bother. They're busy with their own lives, and they figure old people don't have any value anymore. I've learned so much from these people over the years. They are all individuals. They were all young once, and those personalities are still firmly inside those bodies."

"We all age. Nobody is going to get out of this life unscathed, unless they die young. I just don't understand abandoning your family."

She looked around at all the people talking and hugging and laughing and noticed a woman she hadn't seen before standing over near the dock, her arms crossed. She was wearing an expensive looking pale pink dress, and a set of pearls hung around her long, slender neck.

"Who is that?"

Bennett blew out of breath. "That is Dorothy Monroe."

"Why does that name sound familiar?"

He laughed. "Maybe because she's one of the most famous old Hollywood actresses of all time? Dorothy was in thirty-two movies back in her day. She's been living here for about eight months now, but she rarely comes out of her room. She has food delivered when she's hungry, and Morty usually drops her groceries off for her because he was such a big fan."

"Why doesn't she come out of her room?"

"Let's just say that Dorothy still thinks she's famous and deserving of attention. She can have a bit of a prima donna personality, and it didn't sit well with some of the other residents when she first arrived."

Danielle chuckled. "I can totally imagine that."

"She's really a very nice lady, but a little abrasive at times. Kind of demanding. And it appears that she has been stood up by her family."

"Should we go talk to her?"

Bennett nodded. "I think that would be good. She's obviously going to need medical care at some point, so it would be nice for her to meet you."

They walked over to Dorothy, who was still standing there with her arms crossed, her eyes squinting as she stared at the boat. It was as if she was waiting for someone to come off of it and apologize for taking so long.

"Hi, Dorothy. It's good to see you out and about. Were you expecting family?" Bennett asked.

She slowly turned her head and looked at him as if he was asking the dumbest question ever uttered on earth. "Well, do you think I would be standing here staring at that stupid boat if I wasn't expecting someone?"

Danielle was now feeling extremely anxious about introducing herself. The woman was obviously about as welcoming as a rabid porcupine.

"I'm sorry they disappointed you."

She sighed loudly, with dramatic flair. "I don't know why I'm surprised. They dumped me here like some old diseased cat that you put out behind a gas station because you don't want it anymore."

Danielle could definitely tell that she was a creative type. "Hi, I'm Danielle Wright. I'm the island nurse."

Dorothy rolled her eyes. "Pardon me if I don't get too attached."

Again, Danielle couldn't really blame her. She wasn't sure if she was staying, so she had a point.

"Is there anything I can do for you, Dorothy?" Bennett asked.

"Yes. You can dispatch a letter to my family and let them know I will take no further visits or phone calls from them in the future. You can also inform them I'll be calling my attorney to take care of the disposal of the trust funds that I had set up for many of them. I think I'll donate that money to a pet rescue or some sort of homeless cause. Maybe those people would appreciate it."

"Oh, now, I don't want you to make any rash decisions…"

She pivoted her head back toward him, her eyes almost shooting flames. "I pay good money to live here on your island, and I just asked you to do something for me. I expect it to be done."

"I'll ask Naomi to work on that tomorrow. I hope you'll be joining us at the ice cream social tonight?"

"I'm not much for ice cream or social activities. Besides, I'm having dinner brought to my cottage later."

"Well, if you change your mind…"

"I won't." Without saying another word, she turned and started walking away from the crowd and back toward her house, the sound of her low block heels clicking against the paved street. Bennett turned around and looked at Danielle, laughing.

"Wow. You weren't joking. She's as cold as ice."

"Yeah, she's not the easiest to talk to. I have a feeling under all of that gruff exterior lies a woman who's been hurt a lot. It makes me sad."

"You're probably right. The thing is, I'm supposed to be taking care of everybody on this island. I need to set an appointment to see her. Mental health is just as important as physical health."

Bennett lightly patted Danielle on the arm. "Well, good luck with that." He laughed as he walked away, wandering off to greet some of the arriving families.

DANIELLE STOOD in the middle of the gymnasium, looking around at all the families reuniting. They couldn't have the ice cream social in the diner because the space wasn't large enough to accommodate all the visitors. So, they were inside the gymnasium that had a basketball court. What in the world a bunch of senior citizens needed with a big gymnasium was beyond her comprehension.

"Are you not having ice cream?" Naomi asked as she walked up beside her.

"Actually, I've already had both a chocolate cone and a vanilla one. I'm not going to want dinner later!"

Danielle said, rubbing her stomach. She had been blessed with being petite her whole life, so when she overate it looked like she was several months pregnant.

"This is one of my favorite times of the year. I love seeing all of our residents smiling with their families."

"Yeah, it is nice. It makes me sad to see so many people without family here. Like Morty. Who doesn't want to be around him? He's so funny!"

"I know. I would gladly adopt him myself," Naomi said, giggling.

"I'm sorry, Naomi, but will you excuse me? I'd like to go over and meet Gladys' niece."

"Sure. Have a good evening!"

Danielle walked across the gym where she saw Gladys standing with a woman that Bennett had told her was her niece. She was happy to see that Gladys had someone who would come to visit her, given the fact that she was prone to saying a lot of interesting and unique things.

"Hey, Gladys," Danielle said, smiling as she rubbed Gladys' arm.

"Oh, hey, nurse lady."

"Hi, I'm Stephanie, Gladys' niece."

The woman looked like she was probably in her early fifties, very well-made and dressed like she was going to a business meeting. Gladys didn't look overly comfortable with her niece, standing back a few feet and focusing her gaze on her cup of ice cream.

"Nice to meet you. I'm so glad you got to come and see your aunt Gladys. We really enjoy having her around here."

Stephanie looked at her carefully, squinting her eyes just a bit. "Really? It seems like Gladys might be a little... much?" She whispered it, but Gladys could definitely hear her.

"Excuse me?"

"Well, my aunt Gladys has been prone to saying lots of strange things over the last couple of years. It's one reason we chose Wisteria Island for her. We felt like maybe she couldn't take care of herself anymore."

"Which isn't true at all! I take care of my dog," Gladys protested before looking down at her ice cream again.

"Gladys has a very vivid imagination," Danielle said, smiling at Gladys and then looking back at Stephanie.

"Well, she certainly isn't ready to be deciding on what to do with her financial accounts. I was just talking to her about signing over the management of that to me so that I can make sure everything is taken care of."

Danielle had a terrible feeling about this.

"I told you, I'm leaving my money to the Humane Society. I'm not signing anything!" Gladys said before walking off toward the table of ice cream toppings. Now Danielle felt really uncomfortable.

"Sorry you had to hear that, but my aunt Gladys is not playing with a full deck. We've known about it for a couple of years now, and she's got quite a substantial sum of money sitting in bank accounts. She has stocks, mutual funds, etcetera. Someone needs to be taking care of all of that."

"Well, maybe a financial advisor or someone that the court appoints?"

Stephanie glared at her. "I'm her closest living relative. It seems very logical that I should be the one to step up and make sure that money is protected for future generations."

"Gladys never had children, right?"

Danielle realized she was stepping into a minefield that she shouldn't have stepped into.

"Well, I have children. I would think my aunt would want that money to go to them."

"But your aunt is still alive. Who knows how many years she'll spend here on Wisteria Island. Certainly she will need money for that?"

"Are you saying that my hallucinating, dementia ridden aunt should be able to control all of her money?" Stephanie said loudly. Hands on her hips, she waited for an answer.

"Hey... What's going on over here?" Bennett asked as he walked up.

"Your employee here seems to like to stick her nose into other people's business. That's what's going on!"

Stephanie stomped off to corral Gladys again as Danielle slowly turned around, not wanting to meet Bennett's eyes.

"Danielle?"

She sighed. "I'm sorry. It's just that when I know someone is trying to take advantage of an elderly person, I get kind of upset."

"She's trying to take advantage of Gladys?"

"I think so. She wants Gladys to sign over all of her

financials to her. Gladys wants to leave her money to the Humane Society. I happen to think that she should be able to do with her money what she wants."

"But it's not up to us. We have to stay out of that kind of thing."

She pursed her lips and furrowed her eyebrows. "We are here to protect these people. Isn't that what you're always preaching?"

"Danielle, we can only do so much. We can take care of them medically, make sure they have a safe place to live, help them be vital right up until the very end. We can't interfere with their family relationships or mess with their financials."

"I know you're right," she said, relenting. "It's just that I really like Gladys, and I feel like something else is going on."

"What do you mean?"

"I don't know. Gladys isn't exhibiting the typical dementia symptoms. She's not hallucinating per se."

"She sees things that aren't there."

"Yes, but I still think there might be something else causing it. I think I'm going to set an appointment with Gladys and go over her medical history, her medications, that sort of thing. If I can stop all of this perceived dementia or craziness from happening, then she will be in her right mind and be able to take care of her own money."

Bennett smiled. "If I didn't know better, you sure would sound like a woman who's planning to stay here long term."

"Look, I know I'm staying here for right now. I

always strive to do my best at every job. It's just part of my personality. If I can help any of these people have a better life, then I will. I'm not making any promises about how long I'll stay, Bennett."

"Fair enough. Well, I better get back to making my rounds."

As she watched him walk off, she thought more about Gladys' situation. If there was anything she could do to keep Stephanie from stealing Gladys' life savings, she was going to do it.

∼

DANIELLE'S FEET were killing her. When would she ever learn not to wear her fancier shoes? Sure, they looked cute, but they were squeezing her feet something fierce.

"Have you seen my niece?" Gladys asked in a whisper as she came up behind Danielle.

"No, I haven't seen her lately."

Gladys grinned. "Good! I've been trying to lose her all afternoon. See ya!"

Before she could respond, Gladys was gone, apparently hiding from her niece. Danielle couldn't help but laugh to herself at the absurdity of it all.

"Hello."

Danielle turned to see Berta, one of her patients, standing in front of her. "Oh, hi, Berta. How are you?"

"I'm all right, I suppose," she said, staring at something across the gymnasium. Danielle turned to see if she could figure out what it was.

"What are you looking at?"

Berta's face turned a delightful shade of red before she smiled. "Edwin."

Danielle had only met Edwin once so far. He was standing outside of the sandwich shop playing his fiddle, and Danielle had stopped to listen. He was actually quite good, if not a bit quirky. He wore a full wool suit with a fedora all the time, which had to get very hot.

"Oh, you like Edwin, huh?"

"Maybe," she said sheepishly. This was the cutest thing Danielle had ever seen.

"Do you have family here?"

Berta shook her head. "No. My daughter was too busy to come this time. She's a lawyer in Atlanta."

"I'm sorry."

"Oh, it's okay. I've learned how to be alone after all these years. I have my cat, Sassy, and I keep busy with my TV shows and cross stitch."

"But you'd like Edwin to notice you?"

She smiled. "He's the first man I've been interested in since my Louie died twenty-two years ago."

Sometimes, the stories of the people on Wisteria Island made Danielle so sad. On the surface, it was this unique little island full of vibrant older people twirling around at dances and zooming down the pathways on golf carts. When she dug deeper, there was a lot of hurt to be found. A lot of abandonment, lost dreams and wishes unfulfilled.

"Why don't you tell him how you feel?"

She put her hand on her chest. "Oh, dear, no! A lady

doesn't make a pass at a man. I know these days are different, but it's just how I believe things should be done."

Danielle smiled. "I see. Well, can you flirt with him a little?"

She shrugged her tiny shoulders. "I wouldn't have the first clue how to flirt with a man. I was only ever with my Louie, and we were married for thirty-six years."

"Have you spent any time with Edwin?"

She nodded. "We play bingo next to each other every Tuesday and Thursday evening."

"And do you talk to him?"

"Sometimes. We chat about baseball games since we both like that. And he tells me about his grandkids and great-grandkids."

"Good! That's a wonderful starting point."

She chuckled. "I'm seventy-eight years old, Miss Wright. Any notions about Edwin becoming my... friend... are too out there to even consider. It's just a childish crush."

As she watched Berta wander off, she thought about what she could do to help her get together with Edwin. Great, now she was a nurse and a matchmaker.

CHAPTER 8

*B*ennett stared at the files on his desk. How did the stacks get so high when he seemed to always be working? Being a one-man show running an island was a lot more work than one would think. Sure, he could hire more people, but he'd found that the more employees he had, the more stress he had.

"Knock, knock." He looked up to see Danielle standing there. She never showed up at his office unannounced, and he hoped this wasn't the moment she decided to quit and go back to her old life.

"Hey! I didn't expect to see you this morning. I figured you might still be hungover from all the ice cream last night."

She laughed. "Man, that sugar kept me up way past my bedtime. Thank goodness for melatonin."

"Have a seat," he said, pointing to the chair in front of his desk. She sat down. "What's up?"

"Well, I wanted to let you know I'm going to run by Glady's cottage today and see if I can figure out anything that might cause her strange behavior. Is her niece staying with her?"

"I think so."

"I'll have to work around that somehow then."

"Danielle, don't get too involved in family affairs..."

She squinted her eyes at him, a sly smile on her face. "I'm a woman. We know how to manage things like this when we need to."

He chuckled under his breath. "A truer statement was never spoken."

"Anyway, that's not why I came here."

"Then why did you come here?"

"Well, I was chatting with Berta last night, and it seems she has a crush on Edwin. So, I thought you and I could come up with a plan to get them together."

He stared at her. "What?" All he could think about was the enormous amount of work he had on his desk, yet the island nurse wanted to play matchmaker.

"Wouldn't it be adorable?"

"Danielle, we don't offer dating services here on Wisteria Island. I can't believe you'd even have time for something like this."

She sighed and leaned back in the chair. "Don't you have a romantic bone in your body?"

"Of course I do. But why complicate things by having residents date each other?"

"Berta is still a vital woman, and I assume Edwin is a vital man..."

Bennett held up his hand. "Fine. I'll help you. Just stop saying stuff like that."

Danielle laughed. "Great! Dinner at my place tonight."

"What? We eat dinner with the residents, remember?"

She leaned over his desk. "You're the boss. Can't you make an exception for one night?"

He paused for a long moment. "Okay, fine. One dinner."

"Oh, you rebel," she said sarcastically before walking toward the door. "Seven o'clock. Bring dessert."

Before he could say a word, she was gone, and he was left wondering what dinner with Danielle would be like. He would soon find out.

DANIELLE COULDN'T BELIEVE she had invited Bennett to come to dinner at her house. What had she been thinking? She could've just as easily sat in his office for another few minutes and gone over what they could do about getting Berta and Edwin out on a date together. Why had she suddenly invited him to dinner without thinking first?

She opened the oven door and checked on the Italian baked chicken one more time before going out front to get some air. Normally she liked to sit on the back deck and look at the ocean, but she needed to check on the plants in her front flower bed.

Her mother had never been much of a gardener, but Danielle enjoyed planting things. She enjoyed tending to something and watching it grow. The heat was getting progressively worse as summer approached, so she always tried to make sure that her plants had plenty of water each day. She stood out on the walkway, pulling the water hose over to the second flower bed, dousing them with plenty of water before turning off the spigot.

Just as she was about to go back into the house, she noticed Gladys walking alone down the sidewalk with her little white dog.

"Gladys!" she called, waving at her. She didn't normally see Gladys down the road this far, so she hoped everything was okay.

Gladys looked at her and smiled, waving her hand as she walked toward the cottage.

"I didn't know you lived here! I didn't know *anybody* lived here. Isn't this place kind of crappy?"

Danielle chuckled. "It was, but Bennett got it fixed up for me. It's actually pretty cute now."

Gladys scanned her eyes across the front of the house and then looked back at Danielle. "If you say so."

"Where's your niece?"

Gladys rolled her eyes. "Watching some stupid television show that I didn't want to watch. Who watches other people look for houses to buy? I'll be glad when she leaves in a couple of days."

"You don't like having her here to visit you?" Gladys shook her head.

"Just because she's the only family I have doesn't mean I want to see her. She's never been nice to me. Of course, her mother was a horrible person, so that apple didn't fall far from the tree."

Danielle struggled to stifle a laugh. "Listen, do you have a few minutes to sit and have a cup of coffee?"

Gladys stared at her, a smile spreading across her face. "Really? Nobody ever invites me for coffee."

"Of course. I'm having Bennett over for dinner in an hour or so, but I have a few minutes. I need to check on my food. Come on in," she said, motioning for Gladys to follow her.

They walked into the cottage, and Gladys looked around. "This place isn't half bad. It's not as nice as my house but it's livable."

Danielle didn't know if Gladys said the things that she did because of medication, a brain disease, or she just spoke her mind. Sometimes it was refreshing, while other times it was worrisome.

"How do you like your coffee?"

"Black. My mama taught me to drink strong coffee. She said it might put hair on my chest, though I still haven't seen any."

Danielle poured a mug of coffee and set it on the breakfast table. Gladys sat down, still holding tight to her little dog's leash as it laid down on the floor next to her feet.

"What's your dog's name?"

"Her name is Delilah the Dog."

"Hi, Delilah," Danielle said, leaning down to pet the little fluffy pooch.

"No. It's Delilah the Dog. We don't shorten it. She hates that."

"Oh, gotcha. Sorry about that," Danielle said, turning her head to avoid Gladys seeing her smile. Danielle picked up her own cup of coffee and sat down across from Gladys.

"So, are you staying here as the nurse?"

"Right now. I haven't made any future plans."

"Do you have commitment issues?"

Danielle laughed. "What?"

"I heard Dr. Phil talking about it one time. It sounds to me like you have commitment issues."

She had a point. "I don't know, honestly. I've been committed to things before that didn't quite work out."

"So you're scared?"

Danielle reached over and squeezed her hand. "Maybe you missed your calling as a therapist."

"Most people don't stay here because we can be a bit much to deal with," Gladys said, veering off onto another topic of conversation.

"Oh, I like it here pretty well so far. It was a little rocky at the start, but I think I'm finding my footing."

"Good. Glad to hear it." She took a long sip of her coffee and stared out the window.

"So, Gladys, do you mind if I ask you some questions about your medical history?"

Gladys tilted her head. "Why?"

"I just want to make sure you're on the proper medications and that you don't have anything interacting. It's been on my mind."

"Shouldn't I just make an appointment?"

"No need for that. We can do it right here."

Gladys shrugged her shoulders. "Okay. Fine by me."

"Why don't we start by talking about what medications you're currently taking. Do you remember?"

"Well, I take a daily aspirin, vitamin D, B12 shots…" As Gladys rattled off all of her medications, Danielle typed them into her phone so that she could look at them later. There were a couple she wasn't familiar with because they were newer on the market and not something she'd dealt with in the ICU.

"And what diagnosis have you been given about your issues?"

"Oh, I've been told everything from dementia to Alzheimers to just being a little crazy."

"Have you seen a psychiatrist?"

"Honey, I don't remember. I've seen so many doctors over the years. That silly niece of mine is trying to get me to go to some doctor that she's picked out. I know why. She wants him to proclaim that I'm a loony tune so that she can take all of my money."

She had to give it to Gladys. She was very observant of what was going on.

"Do you feel you have memory lapses?"

"Not a lot. I remember to feed my dog, what time Judge Judy comes on TV, when to go to dinner. I remember my childhood. I even remember what I ate for breakfast this morning. Of course, it's the same thing I eat for breakfast every morning - oatmeal with blueberries and bananas. Have you tried that?"

Danielle nodded. "I have. One of my favorites." The truth was, she hated oatmeal, but that wasn't the point of this conversation. "Do you ever feel you see things that aren't there?"

Gladys giggled. "Well, if I see them, doesn't that mean I think they are there? How would I know they weren't there? I mean, if I knew they weren't there, then why would I see them?"

Danielle felt like her head was about to spin around. "I mean, do you sometimes see things and tell others what you see but they don't see it?"

She nodded. "Sometimes. Like I've seen those aliens at the marsh."

"And why are you out at the marsh?"

"I go down there to watch the sunset."

"I see. And you see aliens?"

"Sometimes. They aren't always there."

"Makes sense."

"No, it doesn't. It doesn't make sense at all! I know it sounds crazy, but I see them. I don't like it."

"What do they look like?"

"People think they're green, but they're really not. The ones I see are more gray, and they don't wear any clothes. They don't have the same... stuff... that we have on our bodies. The male ones have these things that look like..."

Danielle realized they were way off track, so she quickly stood up before Gladys could finish her sentence. "Well, I better get working on finishing the food before Bennett gets here. You've given me some great information, Gladys. I'm going to work on figuring out the reason you're seeing things that maybe aren't there."

"You mean you're not going to just write me off as crazy like everybody else has, including my niece?"

She stood up and walked toward the door. "No, I don't think you're crazy. I think something else is going on, and I'm going to help you figure out what it is. I promise. I won't just write you off as crazy."

Gladys turned around and smiled gratefully. "Thank you. It's been a long time since I felt like somebody was in my corner." Unexpectedly, she hugged Danielle before turning and walking down the walkway toward the street.

Suddenly Danielle felt overcome. She felt like she might burst into tears right then and there. Here was a woman who had felt abandoned, alone, like nobody was listening to her. Now she felt comforted that Danielle was in her corner. It was enough to make her cry.

"Have a good night, Gladys. We'll talk soon."

She watched Gladys walk down the sidewalk with her little dog, and she felt pride in her heart that she was trying to fix what was going on with a woman who was basically alone in the world. Maybe she would and maybe she wouldn't, but at least she could go to bed at night knowing that she had tried to do something for a woman who deserved it.

"Whoa! Dinner at Danielle's? How'd you score a date with her? She's a looker!" Eddie said as they rounded the corner in his golf cart. Why on earth he'd agreed to accept a ride from Eddie was beyond him. He always regretted rides with Eddie because they resulted in mild whiplash.

"It's not a date. She wants to talk about work stuff."

Eddie chuckled. "It's been my experience that work stuff is discussed at the office, my dear friend. That lady invited you to her house, and she's cooking? You might as well buy a ring and propose!"

Bennett rolled his eyes. From the day he'd hired Eddie, he'd questioned his judgement. Eddie did a great job, no doubt about that. Still, he was the biggest busybody on the island, and there'd been so many near-misses with him driving the golf cart that Bennett had lost count.

"Don't you go around spreading false rumors about me and Miss Wright."

"Miss Wright. Even the name has 'future wife' written all over it!" He cackled at his own joke before coming to a screeching stop to let some very slow bingo players cross the street. Janice, with her big pink bun, stopped in the road and shook her finger at Eddie.

"How many times have I told you to stop speeding around this island? I swear, I'm going to find a switch and skin your hide, Eddie!" She held up her shiny silver cane and waved it in the air before finishing her walk across the street.

Eddie sheepishly looked over at Bennett. "She has a point."

"Maybe so," Eddie said, as they continued - albeit a bit slower - down the road. "So, do you like Danielle?"

"Of course I like her. She's an exceptional nurse and a nice person."

Eddie looked at him and laughed. "You know exactly what I mean, boss. Do you *like* her?"

"She's my employee, Eddie."

"You're not answering my question." He pulled up in front of Danielle's cottage and looked at Bennett.

"My life is Wisteria Island. You know that. Romantic entanglements are not my thing."

"You're a young guy, Bennett. It'd be nice to see you happy with a good woman and maybe some kiddos."

Bennett smiled and smacked Eddie on the shoulder. "Well, my friend, I've learned that we can't always have what we want. Money definitely doesn't buy happiness and believe me I've tried."

He stepped out of the golf cart and waved at Eddie as he flew off down the road and out of sight. As he looked at Danielle's door, he steeled himself for whatever she had up her sleeve.

"THAT CHICKEN WAS AMAZING! Where'd you learn to cook like that?" Bennett asked as he leaned back in his chair.

"Lots of cooking shows on TV," she said, laughing. "My mother is a terrible cook. Like, she could literally burn anything, and her sense of what spices to use was always wrong. One time, she made an Italian pasta dish but accidentally put cumin in it. Trust me when I say she won't be winning any awards for her culinary skills!"

"What does your mom do for a living?"

Danielle drank a sip of her wine. "She's an epidemiologist."

Bennett's eyes widened. "Wow. That's impressive."

"My dad was a brain surgeon. Ironically, he died of a brain tumor a few years ago."

"I'm so sorry."

"What about your parents?"

"I never really had a father, so we lived a single parent lifestyle."

"Was it tough?"

"Well, I grew up in a single-wide trailer directly across from the town landfill, if that gives you any idea."

"Really?"

"Yep. We were that family that people had to help at Thanksgiving and Christmas. We'd get groceries on our doorstep from strangers, and my toys were always things I didn't exactly ask for. I learned early on that writing to Santa Claus wasn't something I should do because I would only be let down."

"I guess I imagined you grew up in a different situation."

He smiled. "You mean rich? Yeah, not even close. Most of the time, we didn't even have a car. My mom worked two or three jobs and our electricity was off more than it was on. We always had water because we had a well, so I guess that's something."

Danielle had a whole new perspective about him now. "You must be so proud of what you've accomplished in your life."

"You'd think so," he said, taking both of their empty plates and walking to the sink.

"You're not proud?"

He turned on the water and picked up the dish soap, dripping some onto each plate before he started washing them. "I've never really thought about it. My whole life was eat or be eaten, if you know what I mean. Bill collectors calling the house, if our phones were even turned on. People my mom borrowed money from banging on our door at all hours. My grandmother was my only saving grace. She was a saint."

Danielle wiped the table with a wet cloth. "She's the one who inspired this island, right?"

"Yes. I wish she'd lived to see this place."

"You're doing great work in her name. Be proud of that."

He rinsed both plates and put them on the drying rack before turning around and leaning against the counter. "So, what are you most proud of?"

Danielle sighed. "I don't know."

"Oh, come on! You were a highly skilled ICU nurse, right?"

"I *was*."

"Can I ask you something?"

She crossed her arms, a defense mechanism she'd used since childhood, usually to protect herself from her mother's emotional jabs.

"Go ahead."

"Why did you come here?"

She chuckled. "To take a job as a nurse on an island full of crazy people."

"You know what I mean, Danielle. Why leave a prestigious job like that? Something must've happened."

She sighed. "Listen, I'm not a person who enjoys discussing her personal life."

"Oh. Sorry." He walked back to the table and sat down. She paused a moment and then did the same.

"I hope I didn't offend you, Bennett. You're a very nice person, but I'm kind of a closed book. I've never been great at talking about personal things."

He smiled. "And yet you invited me here to orchestrate a love connection for two people you barely know."

Danielle shrugged her shoulders. "I don't like talking about *myself*. Other people are fair game."

"Fair enough. So, what's this big plan?"

"I don't exactly have a big plan. I was hoping you could help me devise one."

"Why is this important to you?"

"I don't know. I guess I want these people to have a second chance. I was watching Berta look across the room at Edwin, and I can't explain the look she had on her face."

"Like she was longing to be with him?" Bennett said, his voice softer than Danielle expected. The moment was both awkward and sweet.

"Something like that."

"What if we just talk to Edwin and convince him to ask her on a date?"

Danielle rolled her eyes before getting up to retrieve the cherry cobbler Bennett had brought. She put it in the center of the table and handed him a spoon.

"That's not very romantic."

Bennett dug into his side of the cobbler, taking a large bite. He'd admitted to Danielle that Esther Wilson had made it. She ran the island bakery, and he felt like no one could do a better job on dessert.

"Okay, so what would you find romantic? As a woman, I mean."

She took a bite from her side and thought for a moment. "Something surprising."

"They're elderly people, Danielle. I don't think surprising them is a good thing."

"I don't mean a surprise, like jumping out from behind their shower curtains. I mean why don't we set up a date and bring them both there."

"How do we know Edwin is even interested?"

She took another bite and stared at him. "Seriously? Edwin isn't exactly a looker, and this island isn't a hotbed of romantic options."

"Still, maybe he enjoys being alone."

"Do you?"

"Do I what?"

"Like being alone?"

He looked down at his cobbler and then took another bite. "Sorry, but I don't like discussing my personal life."

"Touche."

"And no, I don't like being alone."

A long silence hung between them. "I don't think Edwin likes it either," she finally said.

"How about this? We'll set up a romantic dinner on the beach at sunset and then lure each of them there. Thoughts?"

Danielle smiled. "That's actually a great idea. When?"

"As soon as possible. How about tomorrow night? At sunset?"

"Sounds great. I'll get Berta there, and you handle Edwin."

"Okay. I'll get Naomi to help us get the groceries. We'll do it on the beach behind my house."

Danielle grinned. "This is so exciting!"

"I just hope it works or we might have two very upset people to deal with."

She hadn't thought of that, and she wasn't going to. Somebody should have a beautiful romance on this island, she thought, even if it would not be her.

CHAPTER 9

*D*anielle stared at the computer screen. Her eyes were tired, and her hand was cramping. She'd never spent so much time researching medication interactions as she was right now.

Gladys was on several meds, and she'd been so sure that one or more of them was causing the delusional behavior, but so far nothing was showing up. She sighed and slammed her laptop shut. Maybe this was all for nothing. Maybe Gladys just had a neurological issue and Danielle was looking for something that wasn't there.

There had been a time she'd been so sure of her medical skills and intuition. She'd used her gut feelings just as much as her medical knowledge when she'd worked in the ICU. Maybe she'd lost that ability. Maybe she was going soft.

It suddenly dawned on her that she had one trick in her back pocket that might help Gladys. The unfortunate part of that was it was her mother.

Danielle's mother was a world renowned researcher, so she had contacts in every part of the research community. Maybe one of them could help her figure out if the medications were causing Gladys to hallucinate.

She slowly picked up her phone and dialed her mother's number. Steeling herself, she waited for an answer.

"Danielle?"

"Hey, Mom."

"Is everything okay?"

"Of course. Why wouldn't it be?"

"You never call me. I thought something was wrong."

"Nothing is wrong. Can't I just call my mom and say hello?"

Her mother laughed. "That has never been my experience. Are you calling to tell me you're going back to your job?"

"No. I have a job."

She sighed. "How's it going?"

Danielle smiled. "Actually, not bad. I'm getting in the groove of things, and I think the residents are accepting me. Well, most of them. Okay, *some* of them."

"Why wouldn't they accept you? You're a world-class nurse!"

"Said my completely impartial mother," Danielle muttered.

"I can't help that I'm proud of you, Danielle. You should be proud too."

"I don't have much time to talk, but I was hoping

you could help me with something since you have a lot of research contacts."

"Okay. What is it?"

"If I text you a few medication names, can you see if any studies have been done on interactions or weird side effects?"

"Like what kind of side effects?"

"Hallucinations or delusions."

"Why do you need that information?"

"Well, I have a resident who is seeing strange things."

"Like what?"

"Aliens."

"Wow."

"But I think it could be her meds."

"You might be grasping at straws here, dear."

"Maybe so, but I need to know I tried."

"All right. I'll check with some colleagues. I have a friend in Chicago who might know something. Just text the names to me."

"I will as soon as we hang up. Thanks."

"Danielle?"

"Yeah?"

"I hope you know I am proud of you. I just don't want to see you waste your talents or your life. It all passes so quickly. I don't want you to have regrets."

"I know, Mom. I know."

She said goodbye and quickly texted the medication names. It might've been a long shot, but she hoped that her mother would come through and help give Gladys her life back.

~

DANIELLE STOOD at the front of the meeting room. It wasn't large by any stretch of the imagination, but there were only about eighteen residents there, anyway.

"Okay, if everyone could listen up, that'd be great!" she said in her loudest voice. Being so short also meant her voice didn't carry as much as she would like. "Hey!" Her yell finally caught everyone's attention. They looked at the front of the room and stared at her. "Thank you to all of you who came this afternoon to learn more about healthy living. We're going to have a great time!"

"I doubt that!" one woman shouted from the back. Danielle didn't know her name, but she was going to give her special attention.

"Look, I know talking about improving your health sounds really boring, but we're going to be doing some interesting stuff today."

"Darlin', we're all as old as Methuselah! We don't have much time left to improve our health!" Morty said, laughing as he slapped his knee. Today, he was all dolled up in a pink golf shirt, white shorts and a pair of boat shoes that could only be described as neon green. Where he got them, she had no idea.

Most of the crowd consisted of people who didn't have family members visiting. Thankfully, all the visitors would leave tomorrow. There was only one more big event before then - the beach party.

Danielle had been dreading it since they arrived.

Bennett had described it as a cross between spring break and one of those crazy TV talk shows where people threw chairs and yelled obscenities.

He said it started out as fun and games with music and talking, but it often descended into arguments. Yeah, she was really looking forward to that.

"Methuselah?" Danielle said, knowing full well she should've left it alone.

"Good Lord, sweetie, haven't you heard of Methuselah? He lived to be nine-hundred and sixty-nine years old!"

She thought for a moment. "I bet he did it with juicing," she said, smiling. Morty rolled his eyes. "And coincidentally, we're going to talk about juicing and smoothies first!"

As the class moved on, Danielle showed them how to juice vegetables and fruit, explained what they did in the body and then let them try samples. Then she moved into smoothies, and the residents seemed to like those most of all. They also talked about supplements, the importance of exercise, meditation and drinking plenty of water.

Of course, most of that she'd learned online and by taking extra classes. Nursing school had provided little in the way of nutrition or longevity training.

When class was over, Morty approached her. "Miss Danielle?"

"Yes?"

He smiled. "Thanks for this class. No one ever told me those things. For the first time, I think I can actually get a little healthier, even at my age."

"You absolutely can!"

"Do you think I can reduce my blood pressure without the pills?"

"I think it's definitely possible. Why don't we make an agreement?"

"What kind of agreement?" he asked.

"How about we give you a couple of weeks to implement these changes, including a plant-based diet, and then we reassess to see how your blood pressure is doing? If it has gone down by at least a few points, we'll keep those things in place and monitor it a couple of weeks later."

"And if it doesn't come down?"

"Then you agree to try a low-dose of beta blocker and see how you do."

He squinted his eyes and thought for a moment, rubbing his freshly shaven chin. "Okay. I can agree to that." Morty held out his small hand and shook hers.

"Good. I guess you'd better get over to the grocery store and stock up on some healthy fruits and vegetables."

He smiled. "Do I get at least one more plate of fried chicken over at the diner?"

She crossed her arms and wagged one of her fingers at him. "Morty…"

He waved her off. "I was just kidding!"

As she watched him leave, she felt good about what she'd done that day. In fact, it made her feel a lot better to teach people about healthy habits than it did to just keep them alive in a hospital setting. There was very little she could do at the hospital, aside from giving more medication. But if she could help these people prevent the major causes of death, she was making a difference.

She gathered up her things and started walking toward the door, but she caught sight of herself in the mirror on the wall. She had really let herself go since arriving on Wisteria island. Maybe it was because she didn't have to go into a hospital every day or impress anyone in particular. Her hair needed a cut and color, and now was a great time to try out the beauty salon on the island.

"ALL RIGHT, honey, what are you looking to get done?"

Her stylist, Betty Sue, was a tiny little thing with a big bouffant hairdo that was slightly tinted blue. She was dressed like a bit of an artistic hippie, with her baggy tie-dye pants, gray V-neck T-shirt and more jewelry than Danielle had ever seen on one person. Lots of crystals and beads and brightly colored dangly things were all over her wrists and neck. Betty Sue was something else, that much was for sure.

"Well, my hair is getting a little long so I would like a trim and some color too."

Danielle was feeling a little uncomfortable. This place was very much like an old-time beauty shop, unlike the modern salons she was used to back home. There were no big pictures of models on the walls with perfect haircuts and striking make-up. There were just a few chrome salon chairs, mirrors on the wall, and lots of fake greenery everywhere.

"Do you want to cover up these grays?" Betty Sue asked, poking around in her hair like one gorilla would do to another.

Danielle's eyes widened. "I have gray hairs?"

Betty Sue looked at her in the mirror. "Quite a few, darling. You know, women of a certain age…"

Danielle stopped her. "Just go with whatever color you think would look the best on me. This is as close to my natural color as I've been in a while," Danielle said, tugging at the parts of her roots that apparently hadn't already turned gray.

"Okay. Let me go look at what I've got in the back," she said, walking away.

Danielle turned her chair and looked out the window at everybody walking up and down the street. It was a busy day on Wisteria Island as people were getting ready to say goodbye to their loved ones at the beach party. A part of her was looking forward to it, just out of morbid curiosity. She had been to many wild parties in her life, but she was having a hard time envisioning a Wisteria Island beach party being too wild.

Betty Sue made her way back to the chair with a box and started preparing what she needed to color Danielle's hair. Over the next couple of hours, Danielle just let her do her thing, not looking in the mirror very often but staring at her phone most of the time. She rarely had time to peruse social media.

She had gotten a text from Carla that said her job

had been filled. Even though she hadn't planned on going back to that job, there was a part of her that had felt comforted by the fact that she could probably get it back at any time. Nobody had her level of skill and experience, but now that opportunity was gone.

She could get a job at pretty much any hospital in the country, most likely, but that place had been home for a very long time. Knowing that someone else had finally filled her shoes made her feel a little bit lost, a little bit adrift.

She was getting more comfortable on Wisteria Island, but a part of her had always had one foot in and one foot out.

After checking all of her social media, her email, and texting with a couple of friends, she finally put her phone back in her pocket and looked up just as Betty Sue was taking her hair out of the towel. Danielle's eyes almost popped out of their sockets.

"What on earth?" she said, reaching up and touching her hair.

"Doesn't it look beautiful?" Betty Sue stood back and looked at her handiwork with pride.

"It's *red*."

"I know. You told me to put what I thought would look good. Red is a beautiful color!"

"Yes, on a sports car, but not on top of my head! I didn't even have any hints of red in my hair!" Never in her wildest - and scariest - dreams had she considered Betty Sue would make her hair red.

"Sweetie, are you upset? Because your voice is getting awfully loud."

She turned and looked at Betty Sue. "Yes, I'm very upset. I didn't want red hair!"

"Well, you didn't say that. You asked me to pick a color using my expertise, and I thought red was great. You look like a totally different person!"

Danielle felt like she was going to throw up. She looked like she should try out for the lead role as a clown at the circus.

Betty Sue went back to work, blow drying her hair and using a curling iron to style it. When she was done, Danielle wanted to crawl home and hide under her bed. How in the world was she going to go to the beach party looking like this?

Not wanting to cause a big scene, and knowing nothing could be done to fix the problem, she left the salon, went to a local gift shop, bought a huge sun hat, and quickly made her way back to the cottage. She was never leaving home again.

~

BENNETT DIDN'T KNOW why he felt so nervous. In fact, he felt a lot like he did back in high school when he was driving to pick up his first date.

He remembered the moment like it was yesterday. Tiffany Cameron had finally agreed to go out with him after dating her way through the entire football team. Her father, a deputy sheriff, had run every single one of the boys off.

Bennett, who never shied away from a challenge, was determined to impress him. He wasn't so worried about Tiffany. No, he wanted to impress Tiffany's father.

Sure enough, when she came to the door her father was standing behind her, his work gun still holstered on his side even though he was wearing a golf shirt and a pair of jeans. He had his arms crossed, his bulging biceps on full display, complete with the Marine Corps tattoo on his left arm.

Bennett had stuck his chest out like the cocky teenager that he was and strode straight up to her father, his hand out. Tiffany's dad shook his hand and almost broke every bone in it, and Bennett knew he was up against a fierce competitor.

Only two weeks later, he and Tiffany were already over, and she'd moved on to the baseball team. He still felt the same kind of nervousness walking up to Danielle's door that he did with Tiffany. The only difference was there wouldn't be a deputy sheriff standing behind Danielle.

Of course, she was a little unnerving all on her own. He wasn't one who got nervous easily, but something about her always put him on edge. Either he was having butterflies in his stomach or a terrible case of stage fright as he stood before the door of the cottage. Not wanting to lose his nerve, he quickly knocked.

It wasn't like they were going on a date. He had just agreed to bring the golf cart over and pick her up for the beach party. Even though he found her very attractive, he was trying his best to maintain a work relationship.

He knocked again. A couple of minutes passed. He

knocked again. Now he was getting a little worried. Danielle was always punctual, so he couldn't figure out why she wasn't answering.

He pulled his phone out of his pocket and sent her a text. Still nothing. Then he called her, but it went straight to voicemail. He was actually getting concerned now. He peered through the side window next to the front door and then walked a few feet and looked through the window leading into the living room. The blinds were drawn closed, and he couldn't see any light inside.

Unsure of what to do, he walked around to the back to see if maybe he could look into the kitchen window. As he came around the corner, he saw Danielle sitting on the back deck, a large sun hat on her head, and a blanket wrapped around her. He saw a glass of wine with the bottle next to it sitting on the table beside her.

"Danielle?" he said as he slowly approached her.

She didn't turn her head, but instead kept staring straight out at the ocean. "Go away, Bennett!"

He toyed with the idea of walking back to the golf cart, but he just couldn't bring himself to do that when he knew something was obviously wrong with her.

"I thought we were going to the beach party?"

"I'm not going. Go without me."

"Danielle…"

"I said go without me!"

He continued walking slowly toward her, unsure if she was going to spin around and shoot him with a dart gun or something.

"As your boss, I'm letting you know that going to the beach party is part of your job description."

She growled under her breath. "Then fire me because I am most assuredly *not* going." She said the words slowly, like he was someone who needed extra help to understand the English language.

He finally made it to the edge of the deck and walked up the three steps, standing at the top. He felt like if he got any closer, she might actually scratch his eyes out.

"What's wrong? And why are you wearing a hat and a blanket when it's so hot outside?"

"Because I got tired of catching glimpses of myself in the mirror."

"I don't understand."

"Please, just go."

This time, he got a hint of something in her voice. A trembling. The sound of someone who was about to cry. Danielle had certainly not proven herself to be overly emotional in a way that would make her cry.

"Did something happen? Is it your mother?"

"No. This isn't about my mother."

"I'm not leaving until you tell me what's wrong."

She shrugged her shoulders. "Fine. Then I guess you'll just be standing there at the edge of the deck all night because I'm not saying anything else."

Against his better judgment, he slowly sat down on the top step, turning sideways so he could still see her. "Great. I like the ocean." He turned his head back toward the water and closed his eyes, taking in the sea breeze and the sound of the waves lapping at the shore.

They sat like that for a good ten minutes before he was about to completely dehydrate and sweat out of his clothing. He needed a bottle of water and the ability to get more air than he was currently getting sitting down on the deck stairs.

"Do you mind if I go inside and get some water?"

"I don't care."

She truly sounded like she didn't care, her voice monotone.

Bennett walked into the house, shutting the glass door behind him. He walked into the kitchen and retrieved two bottles of water out of the refrigerator. He couldn't help but notice a receipt laying on her counter, so being the curious type, he looked. It was from the hair salon, and it appeared she had left there just an hour before.

Oh, no. Surely she hadn't gone to the hair salon and allowed Betty Sue to do something to her hair. Now he knew exactly what was wrong.

He walked back outside, the extra bottle of water in his hand, and set it next to her. She obviously needed to start hydrating, given the amount of wine it appeared she had been drinking.

"Here, drink some of that. You're going to get dehydrated."

He walked over to the chair next to her and sat down.

"Why are you sitting there?" she said, still not looking at him. He could tell that her eyes were red and puffy from crying.

"You let Betty Sue do something to your hair, didn't

you?" She slowly turned and looked at him, her eyes wide.

"How did you know that?"

"I saw the receipt on the counter."

"I think we should kick her off the island."

Bennett stifled the laugh. "I could've told you to never go to that salon. It's not exactly equipped for your sort of hairstyle."

"Why is she here working on the island, then?"

Bennett laughed. "Look, everybody here has a job. Betty Sue was a hairdresser, as my grandmother would've called it, for many years. Decades, actually. She's not exactly well-versed in the latest modern hairstyles."

"I can never leave here again."

"Don't you think maybe you're just being a little dramatic? You don't strike me as the vain type."

She took the top off of the water bottle and then took a long sip. "Do you like clowns?"

"Not particularly. I pretty much have a lifelong phobia of them."

She almost cracked a smile. "Well, then you're going to love this." Without missing a beat, she took the hat off of her head, dropped the blanket, and allowed her hair to hit her shoulders. It was the brightest shade of red he'd ever seen on top of someone's head.

"Wow."

She smirked. "Yeah, wow. I could've strangled her with my bare hands, but I figured that was frowned upon and might get me fired."

"I am so sorry. Is there anything I can do?"

She put the hat back on her head, this time not being particularly careful about stuffing her strands of hair into it.

"Yeah, you can leave me alone to drown my sorrows. Enjoy the beach party."

"You have to go to the beach party."

"Are you crazy? Did you not just see my hair?"

"Danielle, you have a job to do here. You can't stay in the cottage for weeks on end waiting for your hair to grow out. Besides, these people are going to think it looks nice."

"They're not all blind, Bennett! Nobody is going to think this looks nice except for Betty Sue who needs to see a psychiatrist because she has lost her mind!"

"How about we make a deal?"

"Unless the deal is that I can shave my head, I'm not sure any deals are going to work for me."

He tried to imagine her with a shaved head and then shook the image from his mind.

"You will not need to shave your head. I know there's a great salon over in Seagrove."

"Seagrove? Where is that?"

"We can take the boat to Seagrove Island and then cross the bridge into the little town. I'm sure they can fix this for you."

"That doesn't help me tonight."

"No, it doesn't. Tonight, why don't you wear that beautiful hat and go have a great time at the beach party with your wonderful boss?"

"And you think the salon will be able to fix this?"

"One time, one of the resident's daughters made the

mistake of going to see Betty Sue. She got a terrible perm, and we had to take an emergency boat over to Seagrove to get it fixed."

Danielle started laughing. "An emergency trip for a bad perm? That's something I've never heard before."

"Now, will you go get ready so we can have a delightful time at the beach party?"

"Okay, but if Betty Sue is there, I can't promise that I won't push her into the ocean," she said as she stood up and walked toward the house.

Bennett leaned back in the chair and sighed. Then he burst into laughter, hoping she couldn't hear him.

CHAPTER 10

*D*anielle couldn't believe that she had let Bennett talk her into going to the beach party. As they pulled up into a parking space, she had second thoughts.

"I don't think I can do this."

"Why is this bothering you so much?"

She didn't have a good answer for that. Other than the fact that she had been expected to be perfect for her whole life. Her mother was a fashion icon, even for somebody who should've had nerd stamped on her forehead. Smart and fashionable - it wasn't fair. Then there was her late father, a brain surgeon. How was she ever supposed to measure up to those standards?

When she'd opted to become a nurse instead of a surgeon - which is what her parents wanted - they were visibly disappointed. At her nursing school graduation, they smiled and congratulated her, but she could tell they wanted more. Always more.

Being criticized was something that was her

Achilles' heel. It was one reason she hadn't stayed at her last job after the complete debacle with Richard. She just couldn't have people criticizing and judging her every day.

And now it was playing out on Wisteria Island. Here was a group of people at a beach party, and she was too afraid to walk down there on the off chance that they might see a strand of her new red hair popping out of her hat and judge her for it.

"I don't know. I just don't want people staring at me."

"Listen, most of the people here don't have very good eyesight, anyway."

Danielle laughed and slapped him on the shoulder. "Not funny."

"In all seriousness, we are an island full of misfits. I think you've seen that. Even I'm a misfit."

She looked at him. "How are *you* a misfit?"

"I'm one of the richest men in the world, Danielle. I've chosen to live on an island full of old people that nobody else wanted around. In South Carolina. By myself."

"Yeah, why aren't you living the highlife?"

He chuckled. "Nice try at distracting me, but we've got to get down to the beach."

She groaned loudly before finally stepping out of the golf cart. They walked down the short path, and she could hear the music getting louder and louder. It was mostly seventies disco music with a few sixties songs peppered in for good measure. She realized she wouldn't be hearing any modern day pop songs anytime soon.

"Look at that hat!" Morty said as soon as he saw Danielle step onto the beach. She was terrified he would try to take it off of her head. "Darling, I love it! You'll have to tell me where you got that!"

She smiled. "When I'm finished with it, I'll be glad to pass it along to you."

He leaned in and quietly whispered. "I heard what Betty Sue did. I cut my hair at home just to avoid going to that place."

"How did you hear?"

"Oh, Betty Sue was proud of it. She thought she did a fabulous job, but I can only imagine what you've got hiding under that big straw hat."

"I look like the cartoon version of The Little Mermaid," Danielle said, hanging her head. Morty laughed.

"I don't believe I've seen that film, but I can tell you that there's a fabulous salon over in Seagrove…"

"I already told her, and I'm taking her there tomorrow," Bennett said as he walked up.

Morty nodded. "Thank goodness. We can't have you walking around with a giant hat on all the time. Now, why don't you go over and pick out a hamburger or hotdog that suits your fancy!"

As the minutes passed, Danielle got more and more comfortable. It was obvious that nobody was paying attention to her. They were all having a good time laughing, dancing and eating with their loved ones and each other.

She stood there surveying the group of people before her and realized they were all a couple of decades older than her at the very least. They were footloose and fancy free, as her grandmother would've said. They were having a good time, not worrying about what they looked like or what anyone else thought.

What would that be like? To just live her life without caring what other people thought. She watched Bennett as he worked the crowd, hugging the women and shaking the hands of all the men. He fit in there in a way that was inexplicable. He too was decades younger, but he'd been adopted into this group like one of those news stories where the cat adopted the abandoned baby ducklings.

"Hey there!"

She turned to see Gladys standing there, her niece off in the distance, with a scowl on her face, as usual.

"Oh, hey, Gladys."

"I heard about your hair thing. Betty Sue is an awful stylist. One time she turned my hair this weird shade of blue. I looked like one of those Smurfs from that cartoon in the eighties."

Danielle laughed. "So you heard about it too?"

"Betty Sue has told just about everybody here. If you're wearing that hat because of it, we already know. We all feel just terrible for you."

"I'm hoping to get it fixed tomorrow."

"Well, I guess we all have to learn our lesson. Say, have you figured anything out about my brain?"

"No. I'm sorry, I haven't. I promise that I've got some people working on it."

"Well, I sure hope they're quick."

"Why?"

"Because my niece told me this morning that she thinks Wisteria Island is way too expensive. If she gets a hold of my finances, she's going to take me away from here and put me in some nursing home near her house."

Danielle felt the rage welling up within her.

"What?"

"She told me that this morning at breakfast, as she was packing her bags to go home. She said this place is way too expensive and that I'm wasting too much money out of my estate."

"She actually said that?"

"She did. That woman is a piece of work."

"Well, she's certainly a piece of something," Danielle said, trying very hard not to say more.

"I hope I don't have to leave. This place has been my home for the last two years. I love it here. It's my family now."

Danielle put her hands on Gladys' shoulders. "I'm going to do everything I can. I promise."

She saw Gladys' eyes fill with tears. "I just hope it's soon enough."

"Come along, Aunt Gladys," Stephanie said, giving Danielle a look of hatred. "You don't want to monopolize the nurse's time."

"Oh, she's not monopolizing my time at all. I quite

enjoy spending time with Gladys. And I plan to do more of it."

Stephanie eyed her carefully. "Well, you have a good evening," she said, pulling Gladys away. As Danielle watched them walk toward the street, she wondered what would become of Gladys if she couldn't help her. Would she end up in some old folks' home where she got abused? Would she end up alone where no one understood her?

She simply couldn't let that happen. She had to do whatever was necessary to protect Gladys.

"Having a good time?" Bennett asked as he walked up. He had a hotdog in one hand and a hamburger in the other.

"Are you hungry?" Danielle asked, laughing.

"Hey, I don't limit myself when it comes to the beach party. We only do this once a year, and I plan to go home as full as a tick."

"Well, you're certainly on your way," Danielle said. "Listen, Gladys just told me that her niece is planning to move her off the island to save the money and put her in some nursing home."

Bennett stared at her, almost dropping his food. "What? You've got to be kidding me!"

"I just feel so helpless. I haven't heard back from my mother yet, and I'm not sure what else to do."

"Danielle, you've got to prepare yourself for the fact that Gladys may end up leaving here. It's not what I want, and I'll do whatever I can to stop it. We are not her legal family."

"I wonder if we could become her legal family? Could we adopt her?"

Bennett laughed. "I admire your enthusiasm, but I'm not sure that's a legal maneuver that's possible. Then we look like we're trying to steal her money."

"I just hope my mother can come up with something."

"You're a nurse. You know you can't save everybody."

"I know. I just have a feeling that there's more to Gladys' situation than meets the eye."

"I hope you're right, and I hope you can figure it out. In the meantime, don't be a party pooper! You need to get out there, mingle with everybody."

"Fine. But I'm not ready to give up on that whole adoption thing yet," she said, chuckling as she walked away.

THE MORNING CAME EARLY for Danielle. She didn't have any patients to see today, and the beach party had worn her out. She'd never expected the residents to stay up so late. It was after midnight before Bennett had dropped her off at her front door. Eventually, she had taken off her hat and let her red hair flow in the breeze. It would be the only time in her life she was a redhead, after all.

He would arrive at her house within the hour to take her over to some little town called Seagrove. She looked on the map, and it appeared to be a literal dot. It was a few miles outside of Charleston, and it had its own little sea island right off the coast.

Bennett had explained that he was going to be taking her on an adventure, but all she wanted to do was get her hair fixed. He said they would take the boat and make a day of it, visiting some of the local sites and maybe even taking a marsh tour. She wasn't sure about all of that. She just wanted to have her normal hair color back so she could be seen in public again.

As she poured her first cup of coffee, her phone vibrated on the kitchen counter where she had left it sitting overnight to charge.

"Hello?"

"Hi, dear," her mother said on the other end of the line.

"Oh, hey. How's everything going?"

"Well, I have some news for you. One of my colleagues got back to me about that list of medications."

Danielle set her cup of coffee on the counter and waited for the information to come out of her mother's mouth. "Okay. What is it?"

"Well, the medication she's taking for sleep has a very rare side effect of hallucinations. That is especially true if it's mixed with the medication that she's taking for her thyroid."

"Really? That could be it! So all I have to do is talk to the doctor about changing those medications to see if it makes a difference."

"I just wouldn't get your hopes up, Danielle. It's a

very rare side effect. The medication has an excellent track record and is well tolerated by most patients."

"Mom, don't squash my hope. It's really important that I help this woman."

"I've never heard you like this before. Why is this so important to you?"

"I just hate to see someone get taken advantage of, and that's what's happening in this situation. The longer I'm here, the more I realize that older people need more protection in this world. I'll never look at an elder abuse case the same way again."

"Well, I'm proud of you for that."

Danielle almost dropped the phone. Her mother didn't hand out compliments easily, and she knew she didn't agree with Danielle working on Wisteria Island.

"You're really proud of me?"

"Of course I am! I mean, it's not what I would've chosen for your life, to be working on an island full of older people, but if it's what you want, then I say give it your best."

"Really?"

"Listen, I've had a lot of time to think about this while I sat up at night worried about you. I know what Richard did was a horrible thing, and I just didn't want you to let it stop you from pursuing your career. If you're happy where you are, then I'm happy for you."

She couldn't believe what she was hearing. This didn't sound like her mother at all. "Have you been taking any new medications?"

Her mother laughed. "No. But, I have been seeing someone new…"

"Oh, I see. What's his name?"

"Walter. He's a fellow researcher, and he had a former career as a psychotherapist."

"Wow. That was quite a change in careers."

"It was, but it makes him a great listener and a great counselor. We've had a lot of long talks about this, and I've come to realize that you have to pave your own way, Danielle. My path is not your path."

"I appreciate that, Mom. I really do."

"Well, I better go. Walter is coming to take me to breakfast."

"I'm happy for you. I hope things work out, and I get to meet this Walter one day."

"And I hope you find someone who loves you and supports you. That's the only thing that makes me sad. How are you ever going to find someone on an island full of retirees?"

"Hey, there are some nice-looking centenarians here…"

"Goodbye, Danielle!" she said, laughing before she ended the call.

As Danielle sat down at the kitchen table with her cup of coffee, she couldn't help but smile. Her mother had given her a compliment and accepted that she was working on the island, at least for now. Then she had given her the best news about Gladys and her medications.

It might be a long-shot, but she was going to cross her fingers and pray that the change in medication would help Gladys stop seeing things that weren't there.

Riding in the boat with Bennett had been an adventure, to say the least. It was obvious that he wasn't a trained boat captain, but at least he got them over to Seagrove Island in one piece.

A friend of his had lent them a golf cart for the day, and they immediately went over the short bridge into town. She thought it would be some boring little place with nothing to do, but Seagrove actually impressed her.

It had an adorable town square complete with a bookstore, bakery and even a nice-looking yoga studio. She decided that if they had any extra time, she might want to check out some of those places.

"So, what do you think?"

"It's really cute. I think I kind of expected it to be this backwards country place with nothing to do."

"It's really just a much smaller version of Charleston."

She smiled. "A *much, much, much* smaller version."

Bennett laughed. "Well, at least they have a really great hair salon."

She was suddenly reminded of her Pippi Longstocking red hair. She had pulled it into a ponytail and worn a baseball cap to hide at least some of it.

"Yes, I am thankful for that."

A few minutes later, they pulled up in front of the salon. It was still early in the morning, so she assumed she would be one of the first clients of the day. She was happy about that because it meant they would get more time to explore, or at least she hoped so. Bennett was a busy man, obviously with other business interests aside from Wisteria Island. Maybe he would be too rushed to get back to his office.

They walked inside of the salon, and she checked in. "You don't have to wait around here. I can just text you when I'm finished."

He smiled. "I don't mind waiting. I so rarely get time to just sit and not be bothered by something or someone."

He sat down and leaned back into the soft blue gingham sofa that was sitting in the waiting area.

"Okay. Suit yourself. If the fumes of hair dye overwhelm you, you're on your own."

A few moments later, a very normal-looking hairstylist came out from the back wearing a black jacket and black pants. She looked so professional, a far cry from the outfit Betty Sue had been wearing when she turned her in to a circus clown.

"Danielle?"

"That's me," she said, standing up. She had never been ready to do something so much in her life. Of course, getting her hair dyed again so soon might've caused it to fall out, but that seemed like a better option than walking around in her current condition. It wasn't that she didn't like red hair; she did. But the color red Betty Sue had used on her hair looked more like a crime scene recreation than what a natural red head had.

She waved at Bennett as she rounded the corner and followed the stylist.

"So, what are you looking to have done?" the woman asked as she ran her fingers through Danielle's hair, both of them looking in the large mirror.

"Isn't it obvious? I work on Wisteria Island as the nurse, and I made the mistake of going to the hair salon..."

"Oh, are you talking about Betty Sue? She's a hoot! But a terrible hairstylist," the woman said, laughing.

"She thought this color would look good on me, and I made the mistake of letting her surprise me. I have to say, I was definitely surprised."

The woman, whose name tag said Lorna, giggled. "Well, I can see how that would be a surprise. Did she cut it too?"

"She did."

"You have some seriously mismatched layers here... Poor Betty Sue. I don't think her eyesight is what it used to be."

"So, is there anything you can do?" Danielle asked, hope wrapping itself around every word that came out of her mouth.

"I can definitely fix the cut. I think I can do some color neutralization," Lorna said. She seemed very confident.

"Well, it's either neutralize my hair color or I might go neutralize Betty Sue," Danielle said, only partly kidding.

CHAPTER 11

*I*t took over two hours in the salon to get
Danielle's hair back to some semblance of
normal. It was a lighter brown color now, the gray and
the red pretty much eliminated. As far as she was
concerned, Lorna was a magical wizard with powers
beyond anything she'd ever seen.

She walked to the front desk to pay, but the woman
told her that Bennett had already taken care of it. A
part of her felt uncomfortable with that. They certainly
weren't dating or anything. She left a tip and walked
out onto the sidewalk to look for him, since he was no
longer sitting on the sofa. As she rounded the corner,
she found him standing next to the fountain.

"What do you think?"

He turned around slowly and smiled. "Much better,"
he said, laughing.

"And you tried to tell me I didn't look so bad with
the red hair."

"I didn't want you to quit. I can't take another nurse

quitting on me. I paid for your hair to be fixed since I guess it's technically my fault that Betty Sue still runs the salon."

She chuckled. "Well, at least that's a lesson I won't have to learn twice."

"Are you up for brunch?"

"Absolutely."

"There's a great café over next to the bookstore. Care to grab a sandwich?"

"Let's go!"

As they walked around the square, taking their time and chatting about everything they saw, Danielle finally felt relaxed for the first time in weeks.

She was having more and more days where she didn't think about what had happened to her back at her old job or what Richard had done. Instead of it occupying so many moments of her day, it was slipping away like one of those memories that you know happened but you can't quite connect with anymore.

She had memories like that about her dad. After he'd died, she could sometimes still hear his voice in her head or smell his cologne in a crowd of people. Now, she had to search her brain so hard to feel him again. Memories were weird that way.

When they arrived at the café, they took a table outside and sat down. It wasn't long before a server named Denitra came over and took their order.

"What can I get for you?"

"I think I'll take the chicken salad sandwich with a fruit cup," Danielle said. "Oh, and a glass of water, no lemon."

"And I'll take a Reuben sandwich with fries and a sweet tea," Bennett said, handing the menus back to Denitra. "Thanks."

"You're not really a health nut, are you?" Danielle said.

"Not lately," Bennett said. "I guess I've been under a little more stress than normal."

"About the island?"

"Not really. Just some of my other investments. There's never a dull moment in my life."

"I imagine that having a lot of money also brings a lot of responsibility." Denitra walked over and put their drinks on the table.

"It does. I never want to complain about it because I grew up so poor, but having money doesn't necessarily mean you live a stress-free lifestyle. In fact, I think I'm more stressed out now than I was living in that little trailer park across from the landfill."

"How so?"

"I just feel a tremendous weight of responsibility to make the most of what I have. To grow it, to invest it, to help people with it. I remember when I was growing up, my grandmother used to tell me that God gives everybody certain gifts. She called them spiritual gifts. She said if you don't use them, they can be taken away."

"That's certainly an interesting way to look at things."

"She told me about how when she was a kid, she loved to sing. She was good, being a first soprano. Anyway, she was invited to sing at her father's office Christmas party when she was about twelve years old.

She did a good job, so the local fire station wanted her to sing at their party the next morning. Well, she knew her voice wasn't as good in the morning because of her asthma, but she went anyway, and her voice cracked. She was so embarrassed, she started crying and ran out of the room before she could finish the song."

"How horrible."

"She said she never sang in public again, even though she knew it was one of her gifts. As she got older, she started having trouble with her voice, and one of her vocal cords became paralyzed after a virus. Then she couldn't sing at all."

"Bennett, this is a terrible story. You're really bringing me down."

He smiled. "That story always stuck with me. My grandmother, one of the strongest people I knew, had given up on something she loved because she was afraid of looking foolish. Then she lost the gift. I don't want to lose any of my gifts, whatever they are." He took a long sip of his tea.

"You have many gifts."

His face softened. "You haven't known me all that long. How can you know what gifts I have?"

Denitra walked back to the table and set their food down. Bennett looked up and said thank you before she walked back inside.

"Well, I know you have the gift of patience because I've met a lot of the residents, and you are way more gifted at that than I am."

"That might be true."

She smiled and took a bite of cantaloupe. "And you

have the gift of communication. You like to talk... sometimes a lot."

"Well, I can't help it if some people are hard to get to know, and I have to dig deeper."

"And you have the gift of business skills."

"I think you're reaching now."

"I want to tell you how impressed I am with everything you've done with the island. It was a crazy idea, but somehow you made it work. Those people are happy, and you've changed their lives. Probably extended them."

"Thank you. Still, I think what you're doing is much more likely to extend lives. I just paid for an island."

"You're selling yourself short, Bennett. You cared about people that you didn't even know. You created something that didn't exist before. You should be very proud of that. And I know your grandmother would be."

"Okay, you're going to make me cry," he said, taking a bite of his sandwich.

"Well, I wouldn't want to do that. Why don't we talk about something else?"

"Why don't you tell me why you left your last job? The real truth."

For a moment, she thought about protesting. About pushing him away yet again. But she was growing tired of doing that. Hiding one of the worst things that had ever happened to her was becoming more and more difficult.

"Fine. As you know, I was the lead ICU nurse for a major hospital. Took me over a decade to get that position. I was engaged to a doctor who was the head of ICU for his department."

"You were engaged?"

"Yes. His name is Richard. I don't know that we were ever really head over heels in love, but I'm not getting any younger, and we suited each other well."

Bennett chuckled. "Wow, that sounds really romantic.

She shrugged her shoulders and popped a grape into her mouth. "Romance is for silly books and movies. That's not real life."

He stared at her for a moment. "Do you really think that? That romance isn't real?"

"I just know it's never been real for me. Anyway, long story short I found out that Richard was not only engaged to me but to two other women who also worked in the hospital, one of whom is currently pregnant."

His eyes looked like they were about to pop out of his head, much like one of those cartoons she had watched as a kid. The ones where the eyes would bounce out and the little cartoon cat would pick them up and put them right back in.

"Wow. That sounds like some kind of terrible TV movie."

"It really couldn't be a TV movie unless it ended with me strangling him and pushing him off the roof of a building. Instead of doing that, I came to Wisteria Island."

Bennett laughed. "Well, I think you made the right decision."

"And when I got here, I kept getting calls from an old work friend and my mother trying to push me to go back, and maybe I should have. They finally fired Richard. I could've gone back. That's when I realized that Gladys needed my help. So instead of trying to go back and restore my dignity, I decided to stay here. Try to make a difference. Try to make this all worth something."

"Your dignity? But you did nothing wrong, Danielle."

"I was humiliated."

"Richard should've been humiliated. All you did was pick the wrong man."

She didn't know what to say. "Do you believe in soulmates?"

He thought for a moment and then smiled slightly. "I think I do."

"Really? That seems awfully woo-woo to me."

"Woo-woo?" he said with a laugh.

"The thought of having one specific person out there and you have to find them? Scary."

"I think the idea is that if you're meant to be with that person, the universe finds a way to put you together."

"Woo-woo," she repeated before finishing her sandwich. "So, what's on the agenda next, tour guide?"

"Do you like books?"

"I love books!"

"There's a great little bookstore next door. It's called Down Yonder Books."

"The name is amazing."

"Want to give it a try?"

"Sure. Let's do it."

Bennett flagged Denitra down, paid the bill, and they walked next door to the bookstore. It was adorable, as was everything in the town. What Danielle noticed first was the coffee bar.

"Welcome to Down Yonder!" A woman was setting up a book display near the front counter. She was wearing a bright lime green t-shirt with a sequin palm tree, white capri pants also covered in little palm trees, and a pair of sequin covered sandals that, as anyone could easily guess, had palm trees on them.

"Hello," Bennett said, waving.

"Can I help you find anything?"

"No, we're actually just visiting town today and thought we'd stop in," Danielle said.

"Welcome to Seagrove! Is this your first time here?"

"For me it is. I had an appointment at the hair salon."

The woman smiled. "Well, you look beautiful! By the way, I'm Dixie. I co-own this place."

"I love independent bookstores. Such a dying breed, it seems."

Dixie nodded. "Very true, but we're holding down the fort here." The door opened, causing a little bell to chime. "There's my business partner!"

"Hey, I'm Julie," the woman said, smiling as she waved at them before putting her purse behind the counter.

"Nice to meet you. I'm Danielle Wright, and this is my boss, Bennett Alexander."

"Bennett Alexander. Why does that name sound so familiar?" Dixie asked.

Before Bennett could reply, Julie spoke up. "Because he's one of the richest men in the world. You created Wisteria Island, didn't you?"

He nodded. "That would be me."

"Wow, we feel honored to have you here!" Dixie said. "And if you want to fill up your personal library with our books, we won't stop you!"

Danielle laughed. "Bennett doesn't live in a house with a library. He lives in a little cottage, just like me. I'm the island nurse."

"Well, it just goes to show you can't judge a book by its cover," Dixie said, obviously trying to make a pun.

"Why don't we let them look around, Dixie? We don't need to talk their ears off."

Dixie laughed loudly. "Sorry about that, folks. I get carried away, especially when new people come to town. Take as much time as you want to look around, and just let us know if you need anything."

"I'd love a cup of coffee," Danielle said, eyeing the selection of coffee flavorings on the counter.

"Of course! What can I get you?"

Danielle walked closer to the counter. "I'll take a latte with Irish creme flavoring. Bennett, do you want something?"

He shook his head. "No, thanks. I'm going to go take a look at some of the business books."

He walked away as Danielle turned back to the counter. Dixie and Julie were staring at her expectantly.

"What?"

"What's he like?" Dixie asked, grinning.

"Who? Bennett?"

"Yes, Bennett! We've seen so many stories about him. He's seems so mysterious."

Danielle laughed. "There is nothing mysterious about Bennett. He's just a normal guy."

"He's worth almost a billion dollars," Julie said softly. "He can't just be a normal guy. I'd pass out every time I logged into my online bank account."

A billion dollars? How hadn't she known he was *that* rich? It hadn't occurred to her to look up that information.

Of course, Danielle had never been overly impressed by people with a lot of money. She had been raised by wealthy parents, so it hadn't been something she was particularly focused on. She realized that was a great privilege, and that many people grew up in much different circumstances, including Bennett.

"Well, all I can tell you is that he's a totally normal person. If you didn't read all the news stories, you'd have no idea he had that much money. He does a lot of good with what he has."

Julie finished making the latte and slid it across the counter. "No charge. We like to give visitors to our little town a free coffee."

Danielle smiled. "Thank you. It really is a great town from what I can see."

"You should go up the street and visit my mom's bakery. It's called Hotcakes, and she has the best pound cake you'll ever taste. I think she's featuring strawberry pound cake this week, so I highly recommend it."

Danielle nodded. "We will definitely do that. I have a bit of a sweet tooth."

"What's this about a sweet tooth?" Bennett asked as he walked up to the counter with two books in his hands.

"Julie was telling me that her mom owns a bakery up the street with wonderful pound cake. Care to take a walk and have a little treat?"

"Of course. We want to see everything that Seagrove offers today. We don't get off the island much."

As he paid for his books, Dixie made some recommendations. "We have a yoga studio up the street if you want a challenge."

Danielle laughed. "I don't think Bennett is the yoga type."

"You don't know that!" he said, chuckling. "Maybe I do downward dog every morning."

She looked at him. "Do you?"

"Well, no, but you didn't know that."

Dixie and Julie laughed. "You might also want to go on a marsh tour with my son."

"We were thinking about doing a marsh tour. How do I get in touch with your son?" Bennett asked.

"Here's his business card. He runs tours all throughout the day. They are really informative and fun."

He took the card and put it in his pocket.

"Thank you for all the information and the

wonderful drink. I think we need to go get our pound cake and keep moving. I'm tempted to just sit down in here and read books all day."

As they left the bookstore, Danielle was finding herself feeling more and more at home. The people in the area were friendly and she could see how they would become family quickly if she lived there.

"They were nice," Danielle said as they made it to the sidewalk.

"Yes, they were. That's why I love this area so much."

"Do you ever get tired of people recognizing you by your name?"

He shrugged his shoulders. "There's good and bad with everything. I will never complain about my blessings because I know what it's like to live on the opposite end of the spectrum. So yeah, it's been difficult to know who's really a friend and who is just with me because they want access to my money."

"Not to pry, but has that been a problem in romantic relationships?"

They stopped for a moment and sat down on a park bench. "Why do you think I live on an island with old people? None of them care who I am. They're not impressed by my money."

"But don't you want to live a different lifestyle at some point? On the mainland?"

"Maybe. Right now I'm happy where I am. It's comfortable."

"What do you say we get some of that pound cake?"

He smiled. "I say that sounds like a fantastic idea."

~

AFTER GETTING strawberry pound cake at Hotcakes, Danielle felt like she might explode. She normally didn't eat this much or this often, but she was having such a good time that she couldn't help herself.

"Your turn," she said.

"Okay, let me think… What is your biggest regret in life?"

They'd been sitting on a bench under a huge live oak tree, draped in Spanish moss, watching people as they walked around the square.

"I don't like to have regrets, but I guess if I had one it would be going on a first date with Richard."

"I don't think you should regret that."

She looked at him. "No? And why is that?"

"Because if you hadn't met Richard and found out what a giant jerk he was, you wouldn't be sitting here under a tree with me right now."

Her heart skipped a beat. What did he mean by that? "Bennett, I… um…"

"Relax. I just meant that you've been a great nurse to the residents, so I'm obviously glad you met Richard."

She laughed. "So, you're glad that Richard screwed me over and ruined my career just so I would be forced to flee to your island?"

"Well, when you say it like that, it sounds a bit self serving."

"A bit?" She knocked her shoulder into his. The more time she spent with Bennett, the more comfortable she became. They were definitely friends, but she had to admit that sometimes she felt twinges of *more*. She just wasn't sure what it meant or what to do about it. Dating a co-worker had turned out very badly the last time. She could only imagine what dating her boss would cause.

"Your turn."

"What is your most embarrassing moment?"

Bennett thought for a minute. "First day of middle school. I was a nerdy kid, and I definitely wasn't popular or anything. Didn't help that I wore tattered thrift store clothing. Anyway, on the first day of school I was walking across the cafeteria, tray in hand, trying to find a table. I slipped on a banana peel - literally - and slid under the table, tray still in hand."

"Oh, my gosh! What did you do?"

"I stayed under the table."

Danielle laughed. "So you just sat under the table and ate your food?"

He nodded his head. "I couldn't show my face. I just decided I was hungry enough to stay under there, I guess."

"That's so terrible. I feel sorry for little Bennett," she said, patting his knee without thinking. She quickly pulled her hand back.

"What about you? What is your most embarrassing moment?"

Danielle turned her head and stared at him. "Seriously? Given what I've been through in the last year, you don't know that answer already?"

He bit his lip. "Sorry, I guess I wasn't thinking."

"Excuse me, folks," a woman said as she walked over. She was petite, with more curly hair than Danielle had ever seen in her life.

"Hi," Danielle said, looking up at her.

"I'm so sorry to interrupt, but we're having a free yoga class in a few minutes, so I thought I'd see if y'all might like to attend? It's going to be right here on the square."

Danielle pointed to Bennett. "I don't think this guy is meant for yoga."

He quickly turned his head and looked at her. "You don't think I could do yoga?"

"Oh no, I didn't mean to start an argument…" the woman said.

"No argument. It just sounds like my friend here is throwing down a challenge," Bennett said, looking at Danielle.

"I was just joking. Besides, I'm sure we have to get back home soon."

"It sounds like you're scared," he said. The woman stood there, looking back-and-forth between them as they bantered.

"Okay, fine. I've taken yoga classes before back in the city. Have you ever taken a yoga class?" She crossed her arms and waited for an answer.

Bennett cleared his throat. "Well, no. But it doesn't look so hard."

The woman started laughing. "Famous last words. Don't worry, I will go easy on you. By the way, I'm Janine. I own the yoga studio here. Are you new in town?"

"Bennett owns Wisteria Island. I'm the island's nurse."

"Wow. So, you're Bennett Alexander. I thought you were some kind of mythical creature. I can't wait to tell people you came to my yoga class."

He stood up, smiled, and shook her hand. "There's money in it for you if you don't kill me," he said, chuckling as they followed her across the square.

"Can we please do something more relaxing?" Bennett said as they walked away from the scene of the crime. Well, the yoga class anyway. Never in his life had he sweated so much. Who knew that bending yourself into all of those positions was actually hard work?

"I thought yoga *was* relaxing," Danielle said, chuckling.

"I have to give it to you, you were great at that. Maybe you should sign up for some classes."

"And do what? Hop in the boat a couple of times a week and drive myself over here?"

"I don't mind bringing you. I enjoy coming over here, but I don't normally have anyone to do that with."

He was getting dangerously close to making them sound like a couple. He couldn't help it. She was just so easy to get along with. It all felt so natural, and that was dangerous. He'd never been able to trust a woman, especially since he started making so much money.

But there was something different about Danielle. She wasn't impressed by his money. In fact, she seemed like a person who wasn't impressed by much. It would take a lot of work on his part to impress her.

"Maybe I can get Janine to come over to the island and do some yoga classes. I'm sure the residents would enjoy it."

He noticed anytime he brought up something that sounded more personal, like their friendship, Danielle would steer the conversation back to work. She was probably smart to do that.

"Should we go get some more pound cake? Or maybe one of those cupcakes?"

"After doing all of that yoga? I burned so many calories! Not sure I should ruin it!"

"Come on, you're already in great shape."

As soon as he said it, he wanted to reel the words back in like a fishing line. *He was her boss.* He wasn't supposed to be commenting on her shape, good or bad. Bennett wasn't that kind of guy. He didn't feel like her boss right now, and that was getting into awfully dangerous territory.

"I'm sorry. I shouldn't have said that."

She smiled. "I know what you meant. And thank you. I was really big into exercising back at my old job. We had a nice gym in the hospital."

"Still, I shouldn't have commented on your physical appearance. I've had more than enough training in human resources to know that."

"Relax, Bennett. I think I know who you are. I wasn't offended. I promise I won't sue you."

He chuckled. "So, is that a no on the cupcake?"

"Okay, you talked me into it."

CHAPTER 12

They stood on the dock, waiting for the tour guide to be ready for them. Danielle didn't know what this marsh tour was going to be like. She had visions of alligators leaping through the air and taking off her head. Although she wasn't someone who studied nature, she was pretty sure alligators weren't prone to doing that.

"You guys can come aboard," the tour guide, William, said. From what she had overheard when he was talking to Bennett, he had started the tour guide and charter company very recently. He had grown up in the area, and he knew just about everything there was to know about the marshlands.

"Thanks for taking us last minute," Bennett said as he reached back for Danielle's hand. She took his hand, noticing how firm and warm it was, and stepped into the boat.

They both took a seat while William got the motor

started and they began to weave through the grassy marshes.

"No problem. I'm always happy to go out on a tour. Looking at all of this beautiful nature never gets old."

"It really is a beautiful area. I wasn't familiar with the low country until I took this job," Danielle said.

"I can't imagine living anywhere else. I've left a couple of times, but I always came back home. I'm engaged, so we will be here forever."

"Congratulations!" Bennett said.

"Yeah, she runs the yoga studio in town."

Danielle laughed. "She's the one who almost killed us on the square today."

William looked at them and chuckled. "She kills me regularly."

As they continued moving through the dense marsh, Danielle listened to everything he had to say about the area, the nature and the land. It was all very interesting, and she found herself asking questions.

"You wouldn't believe the population of plants and animals that live in our salt marsh habitat. The tides come in and out each day, breathing new life into the environment. Some people think these marshes are just gross, muddy places, but that's not true. If we didn't have the marshes, many of the animals in this area would cease to exist. There's an entire food chain based upon these salt marshes," William said as they glided along.

Every so often, Bennett would look at her and smile, obviously enjoying the tour. She also got the feeling that he was enjoying her company, and she had to admit she was enjoying his. It felt unnerving, dangerous even.

"How often do the tides come in and out?" Danielle asked.

"Every six hours and six minutes, the tides come in. It almost covers up all the grasses, but it also stirs up the bottom to release more nutrients."

"Wow, very interesting. Isn't it amazing how mother nature just knows how to tell time like that?" Danielle said, laughing.

"What sort of wildlife do you see around here?" Bennett asked.

"We see all kinds of things, including alligators. My favorites are the blue crabs. They scavenge little animals. Then you have the wading birds that have their feasts in the tidal flats by eating crabs, snails and fish. I also see deer from time to time, although they're getting crowded out of their habitat by development, it seems."

They continued moving along with William pointing out all kinds of things. Danielle didn't know that the marshes were so interesting. She just saw them as bodies of water with a lot of grass sticking up. The smells and the sounds and sights of the marsh were every bit as exciting as looking out over the beautiful open ocean.

"The time of year makes a big difference in the salt marshes. Certain things happen in spring, summer, fall and winter."

"Like what?" Bennett asked.

"Well, like in the spring is when the salt marshes

start to green. Insects hatch, the birds breed. You start to really hear the music of the marsh during that time of year."

"What's it like in winter? Danielle asked.

"Well, the cord grass dies, but it builds peat from the rotting stems, and that fertilizes the plankton in the bays and the ocean. You also see raccoons at night as they forage on oysters and clams."

"What is that smell exactly?" Danielle finally asked, waving her hand in front of her face.

William laughed. "Many people ask that question. That pungent smell is something that is quite natural in these coastal areas. It's really a mixture of things. For one, there's the salt water and chlorophyll from the plants. There's a lot of decay that goes on in the marsh as the plants and animals decompose and release nitrogen into the air. Then there's the sulfur which is a kind of rotten egg smell. That only happens when the marsh has been dug or disturbed in some way."

She was amazed at how much William really knew about the marsh. It was like he had taken a master's degree level course in it.

"Something keeps biting me," Danielle said, slapping at her arm.

"Oh yeah," William said, nodding his head. "Those are called no-see-ums."

"No-see-ums?"

"They are little blood-sucking insects."

Danielle felt twitchy all of the sudden. "Like mosquitoes?"

"Kind of, but you can't see them, thus their name.

They can really bite something fierce. Over five million of their eggs are usually laid per acre in the spring and fall."

"Gross."

"Here, spray some of this on you," he said, handing her a bottle of something. At this point, she was willing to spray battery acid directly on her skin if it helped.

"Look over there!" Bennett said, pointing at something.

"Yep, there's an alligator."

Without thinking, Danielle jumped sideways, right up against Bennett.

"Sorry," she said, quietly.

He looked at her, clearing his throat. "No problem."

There was a long moment of awkward silence between them as she slowly slid herself a couple of inches back in the other direction.

"No worries about the alligator," William said, not noticing their strange exchange. "He won't bother us if we don't bother him."

For the next hour, they meandered their way through the marshes until they were finally back at the dock. As they stepped off and thanked William, Danielle couldn't remember a time in the recent past where she had enjoyed herself more. Surprisingly, she had learned a lot and been very interested in what William had to say about her new home.

Her home.

That was the first time she had allowed herself to think of this place as something more than a temporary stop to get her away from the craziness that was her life.

But as each day passed, she thought less of the hospital as her home and more of Wisteria Island.

"Thanks again," Bennett said, turning around and waving at William as they walked away.

"I don't know about you, but I'm exhausted!"

"Yeah, I guess we'd better get back to the island. Our dock is just down here a short way."

"Bennett?"

He stopped and looked at her.

"Yeah?"

"Thank you for bringing me here today. I've been feeling a little lost, like a fish out of water lately, but this place has made me feel like it might be possible to make my home here."

"I'm glad, Danielle," he said, smiling. "I can see you doing really great things on the island, so anything I can do to keep you here, I'm willing."

They started walking again. "I'm curious. Did you take your other nurses on field trips like this?"

He laughed, looking over at her. "Not a single one."

THE ISLAND finally felt normal again now that all the guests had gone. Well, whatever normal was for Wisteria Island.

She never would've admitted it to anyone out loud, but she couldn't stop smiling after her day of fun with

Bennett. *He was her boss.* This was a fact that she had to remind herself of repeatedly.

He sure didn't feel like her boss. He felt, at the very least, like her friend. Opening herself up to trusting anyone again seemed just about as safe as jumping into that marsh next to an alligator.

Bennett was a different kind of guy, despite his wealth. In fact, if she were listing the kindest people she had ever met, he would be near the top of the list.

A couple of times during their outing, she had found herself smiling and having butterflies in her stomach like she was a high school girl about to go out on her first date. This was dangerous territory, and she knew it. She couldn't stop thinking about how well they had gotten along, and how much fun she'd had.

Even when she had dated Richard, fun wasn't really their thing. They talked about work a lot, and they occasionally went out for expensive dinners and bottles of wine. One time, he had taken her to an art gallery opening, and when she had complained how boring it was, they'd gotten into a big argument.

Never in his life had Richard ever been on a marsh tour. He certainly wouldn't have known how to take a boat to an island. In fact, he had a maid, a driver and a staff of people that waited on him hand and foot when he wasn't at work. To say that he had a God complex was an understatement.

"Dorothy?" Danielle called as she knocked on Dorothy Monroe's front door. She had been putting off visiting her for days now. The woman was a bit scary, and Danielle wasn't easily intimidated.

There was no answer, but she knew Dorothy was inside. She knocked on the door again, calling her name.

"Dorothy, it's Danielle, the nurse. I'm not going away."

Still, nothing. For a moment, she started to worry. This was, after all, an island full of older people. What if she had passed away inside? It wasn't like she had a lot of friends on the island who were coming by to check on her regularly.

Just as she was about to text Bennett to ask him what to do, she heard someone moving around inside. The door lock clicked, and Dorothy opened it, standing there with the most unwelcome of looks on her face. She was wearing a long flowy nightgown with a gold and pink pattern and big bell sleeves.

"Oh, good. I was beginning to worry."

Dorothy stared at her for a moment. "You thought I was dead, didn't you?"

"Can I come in?"

She sighed loudly. "Suit yourself."

She stepped back, and Danielle walked into the living room. The place was decorated like something out of an old Hollywood movie, everything shiny and gold. Lots of mirrors. Vintage red sofas. She wondered how Dorothy got all of this to the island in the first place.

"Wow, you have a beautiful place here."

Dorothy walked around her and over to the sofa, sitting down. She pulled a cigarette out of the nearby package and lit it up. Danielle was definitely against smoking, but she couldn't help but notice how cool Dorothy looked doing it. Like an old Hollywood starlet from back in the day before cigarettes were known to be unhealthy.

"Thank you. I had to hire a special transport boat to bring my things here when I moved."

"Well, it's lovely," Danielle said, sitting down in a chair.

"What are you doing here?"

"I just wanted to reach out to you since I haven't had an appointment with you in the office. I want to provide the best healthcare possible to all the residents of Wisteria Island."

"I'm not sick."

"Of course. I can also help you improve your health. I had a health expo the other day where we talked about juicing, smoothies…"

"I'm not interested."

Danielle suddenly felt like she was a door-to-door salesperson being turned away.

"But wouldn't you like to learn about how to have more longevity?"

Dorothy laughed, more like a cackle. "Why in the world would I want to stay on this earth any longer than is necessary?"

"Excuse me?"

"Look, I know you're young, but I'm not. Most everyone I have ever loved is already dead. If I didn't think I might end up in the fiery pits of hell, I would exit the planet as quickly as I could."

Danielle had never been speechless, but she was

right now. She had no idea what to say about that, and a part of her felt deeply troubled by what Dorothy had just said.

"Dorothy, are you at risk of harming yourself?"

She rolled her eyes. "If I wanted to harm myself, I would've already done so. I don't need you telling me what to do."

"I'm sorry about your losses."

"I also don't need your pity."

She had never seen someone with such a hard shell before. Obviously, a lot had happened to Dorothy in her lifetime that Danielle would probably never know. She was only there to provide medical care, and how could she do that if her patient didn't want her help?

"I don't pity you. I was just expressing condolences for your loss."

"Look, I know you're trying to help, but I'm just waiting at this point."

"Waiting?"

"Waiting to die."

"Dorothy, there can be so much more to your life."

She looked at Danielle and laughed under her breath. "Very easy for a young person to say. I'm tired. Tired of being alone. Tired of having nothing to do. Just plain tired."

"Have you tried getting involved on the island? There's so much to do here."

"I don't want to square dance or play shuffleboard or go to bingo night. That's old people stuff."

"Old people stuff?"

"What you'll find out when you get my age is that

your mind stays the same. I was something else when I was younger. Everyone looked up to me. Magazines took my picture. Directors sought me out for movie roles. So in my mind, that's who I am. When I look in the mirror every morning, I don't recognize who I see. She looks tired and worn and wrinkled."

"I wish I knew what to say."

"There's nothing to say. You see, this isn't about drinking a smoothie or finding a hobby. It's about living a life. When everyone you love is already gone or has abandoned you, and you're on an island full of people who are nothing like you, you find yourself unmotivated to do anything to change that."

"And your family didn't come to visit you."

"Yes, I have to say that was rather bothersome. They certainly enjoy spending my money, but they couldn't take time out to come see me. Most of my life, I was a commodity. I was never really seen for my true nature. I was pretty, and that was all anyone saw. I was a character, and I played that character well. It didn't exactly lead to strong relationships with people."

"Can I ask you which family members were supposed to come visit you?"

"I have two nieces. I thought they would come, even though they never responded to my invitation. I suppose part of it is my fault, really. I wasn't your traditional aunt."

"Is there anything I can do for you, Dorothy?"

"I don't think so. If I have a health issue, I'll be sure to reach out."

"Okay. I'll leave you alone then. I do hope you'll take part in some of the activities on the island, though."

Danielle stood up and walked toward the door, Dorothy following her. "It's no use. People here already don't like me."

"I find that people here are very forgiving. They didn't like me at first either, and some of them probably still don't. Each person here has their own baggage, and it might take them some time to warm up to you. A little piece of advice from a younger person who probably has no business giving it, but maybe this is an opportunity for you to show people who you really are instead of playing that character you were talking about. You can change your life as soon as you change your mind, Dorothy."

Dorothy said nothing and let her out of the front door, closing it quietly behind her. She wasn't sure that she had done anything of significance by going to visit, but at least it made her feel better that she had reached out. Still, she left there feeling sad for a woman who felt so alone and betrayed.

CHAPTER 13

*D*anielle sat nervously, her hands in her lap, as she waited for the doctor to finish writing his notes in the other room. Gladys, sitting next to her, also seemed a little more jittery than normal. Perhaps she understood the gravity of what the doctor was assessing with her brain health. A part of Danielle was worried she'd gotten Gladys' hopes up.

They had spent most of the day over in Charleston at a specialist's office. Her mother had put her in touch with someone who had put her in touch with someone else who had led her to a neurologist that specialized in the types of problems Gladys was having. It had definitely involved a long train of people to get to this point.

He had done many tests that day, including an MRI and some kind of new brain imaging that Danielle hadn't even seen before. He had also gone over the information about her medication, and in the next few minutes he would hopefully walk through the door and be able to shed some light on Gladys' situation.

"What if those tests show that I really am crazy?" Gladys said.

Danielle squeezed her knee. "Don't you be thinking like that. You're a smart lady, Gladys. You're most certainly not crazy."

Jeremy, the island's resident boat captain, had taken Gladys and Danielle over to the mainland earlier in the day. From there, a rental car was waiting so that Danielle could drive them into Charleston. It was a long drive, but she and Gladys had made the most of it by listening to music and a little bit of talk radio.

It had actually been pretty fun to listen to Gladys' thoughts on the different topics that came up on those talk radio shows. She was a lot smarter than her niece was giving her credit for, and she just didn't seem like somebody who was losing her mind at all.

Still, Gladys had a vivid imagination, and she apparently saw things that weren't there sometimes. That was the problem. Her niece could definitely use that to have her deemed unfit to care for herself so that she could take control of the money.

Bennett had offered to come with them, but Danielle didn't want it to appear that she was spending a lot of her free time with her boss. The whole thing was making her more uncomfortable, but that was probably because she felt an attraction to him. No matter how hard she tried to deny it, it was there, it was real, and it was overwhelming at times.

"Sorry to keep you waiting, ladies," the doctor said

as he walked into the office. He set a file on the desk, turned on his iPad, and then sat down in the chair across from them.

So far, Danielle had found Dr. Lambert to be highly qualified, professional, and very kind. Even when Gladys explained the aliens to him, he sat there with a straight face like nothing strange was going on.

"No problem. We don't have anything else to do," Gladys said offhandedly. Danielle thought about all the appointments she had canceled that day just to be with Gladys for these tests. She definitely had things to do, but Gladys was always at the top of her list.

"Well, let's start with your MRI. Everything was normal. I saw nothing out of the ordinary for someone your age."

"That's wonderful to hear. Isn't it, Gladys?"

"I kind of feel like he might have just called me old," she said, squinting her eyes at him.

Dr. Lambert chuckled. "Not intended that way, Gladys. So the other brain imaging scans we did showed over activity in certain parts of the brain related to creativity and anxiety."

"What does that mean?" Gladys asked.

"Well, it seems like your brain is fighting itself sometimes. You are extremely creative, but the anxiety centers in your brain are also trying to be the star of the show, so to speak. So I think you're getting your wires crossed when you get anxious, and you get these overly creative visions in your head."

"So I am crazy?"

"No, certainly not. When I looked at the medication

interactions, it seems very clear to me that this could be caused by those medications. So what I'd like to do is take you off of these two medications," he said, pointing to his notes as he slid them across the desk. "We have some better options that will not result in these kinds of interactions and symptoms. We will give those a try for a couple of weeks and see how you do."

"So you feel like this might be reversible?" Danielle asked.

"I feel very confident that it is reversible. So you might not see your beloved aliens much longer, Gladys," he said with a wink.

"Oh, that's good. You know, they're quite ugly."

"I'll have my nurse write out the prescriptions for you. For now, completely cease those two medications. You can start the new thyroid medication today. Definitely don't take any more of the sleep medication."

"Thank you so much, Dr. Lambert. This gives us a lot of hope that Gladys' life is about to get better."

He smiled and walked out of the room. Gladys looked at Danielle and grinned.

"So does this mean that my niece isn't going to make me move?"

"If we can get you feeling better, there's not a lot she's going to be able to do because you are completely in your right mind. In fact, I bet the doctor will write us a letter to that fact."

Gladys hugged her tightly. "Thank you. Thank you so much for helping me."

"So, it looks like Gladys might get a new lease on life?" Bennett asked as he took another bite of his shrimp.

After Gladys' doctor appointment, Bennett had called and asked if Danielle might want to meet for dinner at a restaurant in Seagrove. It sat right on the water overlooking the marsh, with plenty of outdoor dining. She sent Gladys back across to the island with Jeremy, and then Bennett met her a little later.

"I think so. The doctor sounded really hopeful."

"That's amazing. You've really made a big difference in her life, Danielle. I'm proud of you."

Something about that struck her. Very few people in her life had ever really been proud of her, and it warmed her heart to hear him say it.

"I hope it all works out. Gladys is a wonderful person. She tells it like it is," she said, laughing before taking a bite of her grilled chicken. Danielle wasn't a big fan of seafood.

"So, when are we going to plan the date for Berta and Edwin?"

She smiled. "Well, I wanted to talk to you about that. I was thinking maybe tomorrow night?"

"Okay. I'll have Naomi pick up the groceries that we need and take them to my house. If you want to come over after work, we can start setting everything up and then get the two lovebirds together."

Danielle rubbed her hands together. "This is going to be so fun!"

At that moment, she realized just how much her personality had changed since she had come to Wisteria Island. When she worked at the hospital, she was a much more serious person. Never would she have thought about fixing two people up on a date. She was far too busy just trying to keep her head above water.

With a relationship that was faltering, and a job that had her working at least sixty hours a week, she hadn't had much time for joy. Wisteria Island allowed her to have a little joy each day.

"You have a pretty smile," he said softly. Then, his face fell a bit.

"Thank you."

"I don't know why I keep saying things like that. I'm really sorry."

Danielle started laughing. "Are you scared I'm going to take you to court or something?"

"This is hard."

"What's hard?"

He sighed and put down his fork. "I'm not going to lie. I am attracted to you, Danielle."

Her heart rate quickened. "Oh."

"And I know it's not okay because I'm your boss, and I'm coming from this level of power over you as an employee…"

"Bennett, I'm not being held hostage or anything."

"I know. I just don't want to do anything to make you uncomfortable."

"I appreciate that. I would be lying if I said I wasn't attracted to you as well."

"Really?"

"But…"

"I figured there was going to be a but."

"I just got out of a really rough relationship that messed me up. I'm just getting on my feet again, so I don't think it's a good time to…"

He held up his hand. "Say no more. I get it. I do. That's not why I wanted to have dinner. I just enjoy your company."

She smiled and nodded her head. "I feel the same way."

As they finished eating dinner, chatting about this and that, Danielle wondered if she was making a huge mistake not pursuing something with Bennett. Maybe he was her soulmate, even though she didn't believe in that sort of thing. There was a part of her that felt like there was a lock on her heart and somehow he had the key. It sounded cheesy, even when she thought about it, but it sure felt true.

BENNETT UNFOLDED the large red and white checkered picnic blanket. "What about this?"

Danielle stared at him. "Do you really think Berta is going to get down on the ground and back up again? You know she has a bad knee!"

He nodded. "You're right. I totally forgot. I think I have a little folding table in my storage closet. Let me go check," he said, walking to the other side of the cottage.

"I'm going to step out onto the deck and get some fresh air."

Danielle had been at his house cooking all morning.

So far, she had made fettuccine Alfredo, side salads and sweet tea. Now she was starving and had no dinner plans. Maybe she'd go home and make a sandwich.

As she stared out at the ocean, she closed her eyes and took in a deep breath. It was hard to imagine living somewhere that didn't have that view. How had she lived so many years staring out her window at a sea of high-rise buildings and shopping centers?

"How about this?"

She turned around to see Bennett standing there with a table in one hand and two folding chairs draped over his other arm.

"Perfect!"

"They should be here soon. We'd better finish getting everything set up."

They had to work quickly, and just as Edwin arrived, Bennett put the last fork on the table. Danielle was pretty proud of what they'd done. There was the table, outfitted with the picnic blanket as a tablecloth, white plates, wine glasses, and two tiki torches lit beside the table.

"What's all this?" Edwin asked as he walked onto the beach.

"I told you I was inviting you to dinner," Bennett said.

Edwin walked over and looked at the table, his hands on his hips. "With candles?"

Bennett laughed. "I might have lied a bit."

"What?"

"You see, Edwin, we heard that someone likes you and has been afraid to tell you."

"Who?"

"Berta."

He sucked in a breath and thought for a moment. "Berta? Really?"

"She's got a bit of a crush. So, we invited her to dinner, and we were hoping you two might hit it off," Danielle said.

"She is a pretty lady…"

"So you'll have dinner with her?"

"You know, I haven't been on a date since before I married my wife, God rest her soul. She died three years ago, and we were married for forty-one years. I'm not sure I know how to do this."

Bennett put his hand on Edwin's shoulder. "It's like riding a bike."

"Here she comes," Danielle whispered when she saw Berta walk over the dunes.

"What's going on?" Berta asked nervously.

"Well, I… I was wondering if you'd like to have dinner with me?" Edwin said.

Bennett and Danielle stepped back a bit to let them have their moment.

"Really?"

"Sure. What do you say?"

She beamed. "That sounds nice, Edwin. Thank you."

He pulled out her chair before sitting down himself. Danielle had never seen anything so cute in her life.

"We'll start bringing your food out shortly," Bennett said as they quickly made their way into the house.

"Oh, my gosh! Was that not the most adorable thing

you've ever seen?" Danielle gushed after making sure Bennett had firmly closed the back door.

He laughed. "I have to say it was pretty cute."

"We did it!" Danielle said, hugging him without thinking. Once she had her arms around his shoulders, his arms slid around her waist. Then time stood still. Neither of them moved. It was the best hug, if not the most awkward, she'd ever had. "Sorry," she said, pulling away.

"I'm not," he said softly.

"We'd better get this food out there."

"Right."

For the next half hour, they served the food, over-hearing Edwin and Berta's conversation. They talked about growing up, their marriages, their kids and their grandkids.

Turned out, Edwin's grandson was a fairly famous Hollywood actor, and Berta used to do modeling in her teenage years. Danielle was learning a lot about them, but it was also a great way of distracting herself after hugging Bennett.

"Here's dessert. I hope you like peach cobbler," Bennett said, setting their plates down.

"My favorite," Edwin said.

"Mine too," Berta replied, looking at Edwin. Yeah, this was a definite love connection.

"Do you need anything else?" Danielle asked.

Edwin cleared his throat. "I don't want to be rude because you two have done so much, but can we be left alone now?"

Danielle stifled a laugh.

"Of course. You two crazy kids behave yourselves," Bennett said, laughing. "Care to take a walk?"

Danielle nodded. "Sure."

They turned and headed down the beach toward her cottage. For the first few minutes, they said nothing, just walking in silence with the ocean waves as their backdrop. It was almost sunset, although if they wanted to see it, they needed to look toward the marsh and not the ocean.

"That was fun," Bennett finally said.

"Yeah, it was."

"Listen, about that hug…"

"I'm sorry, Bennett. I shouldn't have done that."

He stopped. "Danielle?"

"Yes?"

"Are we friends?"

"I think so."

"Friends hug, right?"

"They do," she said, smiling slightly.

"Then stop apologizing. You can hug me anytime."

"I'll keep that in mind," she said, laughing as they started walking again.

"So, do you think we made a love connection?"

She stopped again. "What?"

"With Edwin and Berta."

"Oh. Yes, I think so."

They started walking again. "It's good to know it's never too late."

"Why? Do you think it's too late for you?"

"I'm starting to," Bennett said. He stopped and sat down on a small outcropping of rocks.

"Why do you think that?" she asked, sitting down next to him.

"It just feels that way. It's hard to know the motives of the women I date. My bank account makes me very attractive, but it also makes me very untrusting."

"I can see how that might be a problem."

"Except with you."

"What?"

"You seem unimpressed."

"Well, I grew up with money. I mean, not on the level you have it, but I guess money isn't something that attracts me to a person."

"You dated a doctor," he said, chuckling.

"But not because of money. It was more out of convenience and a shared interest in our career paths."

"Again, super romantic."

Danielle laughed. "I won't ever get a job writing greeting cards, will I?"

"Probably not."

"You know we can't do this, Bennett."

"Do what?"

She looked at him. "*This.*"

He was silent for a moment. "Why?"

"Because it's a bad idea, and you know it."

"I don't know that."

Danielle smiled. "Look, I'm not going to lie and say I don't have feelings for you, Bennett, because I do. Strong ones that I don't know what to do with." *Why was she being honest?* That was only going to lead to uncomfortable conversations.

He turned slightly and looked at her. "Then why not give this a shot?"

"How is it going to look if I'm dating my boss?"

"Fun?"

Danielle smacked him on the arm. "Be serious."

"Look, this is the least judgmental place you'll ever live."

"Are you kidding me? It's taken forever to get them to trust me even a little bit."

"They aren't trusting, but they also aren't judgmental. Nobody cares if we date, Danielle. The only person who cares is you."

She turned back toward the water and stared. "Richard really messed with my head. I'm not sure I'd be good for anybody right now. I can't afford to mess this job up, Bennett." He chuckled. "And why is that funny?"

"Because it means you care about your job, and I never thought that would happen."

She laughed. "Me either."

"Look, I would never do anything to mess up your ability to do your job."

"And what if this ends badly?"

"It won't. No matter what, our relationship will never affect your job. I promise."

She stood up and walked toward the water, allowing it to lap at her feet. Bennett followed her.

"If we do this, it would be a big risk."

"And what if we don't do it? What if we're meant to be together, Danielle?"

She turned and looked up at him, her heart

pounding in her chest. "You know I don't believe in that stuff."

"Well, maybe I believe enough for the both of us," he said. Then it happened. The thing she had wanted to happen in her heart, but was too afraid would happen in her mind.

He kissed her. And it was a good one. Warm and welcoming and felt like home.

When they pulled apart, his hands still on her cheeks, he stared down at her.

"Was that okay?"

She smiled. "I'm not sure. Let's try that again and see."

It seemed like they'd been together forever, and yet everything felt completely new. Danielle didn't know what to make of any of it, only that she didn't want it to stop.

Nothing had ever felt this way with Richard. It always felt forced, monotonous. In this moment, she questioned herself as to why she would've ever settled for anything less than *this*. She didn't even know what to call this. She'd never experienced it before.

They finally came up for air yet again, both of them laughing.

"Woo hoo!" They heard someone say. They turned around to see Morty jumping up and down and clapping about twenty feet away from them.

"Morty! You shouldn't be eavesdropping on people!" Bennett said, wagging his finger.

Morty grinned from ear to ear and did a little dance. "I knew this was going to happen! I knew it!"

"Go away!" Bennett yelled back to him, waving his hand. He watched Morty as he trotted away, walking his little brown fluffy dog further up the beach. "Sorry about that."

Danielle giggled. "It's okay. It's Morty. Did you expect anything different?"

"What do you say we go get something to eat?"

"That sounds great."

He reached out and took her hand as they turned and walked toward the street, and Danielle knew she was in trouble.

CHAPTER 14

*D*anielle could hardly think of anything else, and she really needed to focus on her work. She had already seen three patients that morning, but thankfully nothing too serious. One lady with a urinary tract infection, a man who needed a refill on his blood pressure pills, and a woman who had an ingrown toenail. That one had been pretty disgusting.

The rest of her afternoon would be free, and she was looking forward to the date she had with Bennett that night. They had been spending a lot of time together recently, mostly eating lunch and dinner, taking walks on the beach and talking about their lives. Tonight, he said he had a surprise for her, and she couldn't wait to see what it was.

"Hello? Is anyone here?"

Danielle walked into the waiting room and was surprised to see Dorothy Monroe standing there. As always, she was fashionably dressed, this time in a royal blue pantsuit with a big gold brooch on the lapel.

She had her nails painted a vibrant red and was wearing a large diamond ring Danielle was certain had to be real.

"Dorothy? Did you have an appointment today?"

"No, I didn't. I hope it was okay that I came by to see you?"

"Of course. Come on back and we'll go to room two."

Dorothy followed her into the back and then walked into the examining room, sitting in the chair rather than on the table.

"What can I help you with?"

"Well, I've been thinking a lot about our visit a couple of weeks ago."

"Really?"

"I realized maybe I do need some help."

"What kind of help?"

"I think I'm depressed. I understand that there may be some medication that can help me with that?"

"Absolutely. Why don't I schedule an appointment with a psychiatrist? You can actually do it over video chat."

"What is video chat?"

"I can come to your house and help you set it up so that you can talk to the psychiatrist on your computer. If they think you need medication, they will prescribe it."

"Can't you just do it?"

"I would if I could, but medications for mental health are really best prescribed by a psychiatrist because they're trained in that sort of thing. They'll be able to help you with dosages. I promise to find you someone wonderful."

"But I don't want anyone to know that I have this problem. I am sort of famous, you know."

"Doctors are held to a high standard, Dorothy. They are not allowed to reveal your personal medical information or they could get sued, not to mention lose their license. No worries about anyone ever finding out your personal business."

She thought for a moment and finally nodded. "Okay, let's do that."

"I'm so proud of you, Dorothy! You're taking a step in the right direction. I will come by in the next couple of days and help you get things set up and let you know when the appointment is. Sound good?"

"Yes."

Dorothy stood up and started walking to the front door. She turned around and looked back at Danielle.

"I should say thank you. Most people give up on me very quickly because I can be a bit high maintenance," she said with a slight smile.

"That's all right. I can be a bit high maintenance, too," Danielle whispered loudly. She watched Dorothy wave and then walk outside, moving down the sidewalk alone. It made her sad when she thought about the fact that this woman had walled herself off to so many people. She hoped that medication and counseling would help Dorothy get a new start, even at her age. She deserved to suck every bit of happiness out of life that she could, just like anyone else.

~

"DON'T LET ME FALL!" Danielle said as Bennett led her toward the surprise. They had ridden all over the island on the golf cart with her blindfolded, putting her very close to getting carsick. Bennett didn't want her to know the surprise, so he purposely confused her by driving all around. Now, with his hand on the small of her back, he carefully led her inside of a building.

"I would never let you fall."

Danielle now understood what swooning meant. When people would say that they swooned, she never really understood it. Since going out with Bennett for the last couple of weeks, she understood better than ever.

There was a part of her that didn't want to be this vulnerable. The last time she had trusted someone, they had violated it in a big way. She was realizing that it wasn't fair to compare Bennett to Richard. They were totally different people, and she felt safe and comfortable with Bennett.

"Okay, we can take off your blindfold!" The happiness in his voice almost made her tear up. He was so excited to surprise her.

Danielle reached around and untied the blindfold, pulling it away from her eyes. There were lights everywhere, so it took her a moment to readjust, but then she recognized where they were - the island's only bowling alley.

"We're going bowling?" she said, laughing.

"You don't enjoy bowling?"

"I like bowling. I'm just not very good at it!"

"What size shoe do you need?" Janice, who she remembered from square dancing, asked.

"I wear a size six and a half."

"Good Lord! Let me go check and see if we have shoes that small."

Janice walked away. "I'm sure she can find something."

"So do we have the whole place to ourselves?"

Bennett nodded. "One of the perks of owning the island."

They walked over to lane number three and Bennett sat down to put their names into the computer. The bowling alley was surprisingly high tech, much like one on the mainland.

When Danielle looked up, she noticed he had put her name in as Dani. For some reason, that didn't bother her anymore. She wasn't nearly as straight-laced as she had been when she arrived on the island.

"Here you go!" Janice said, handing a pair of shoes to Danielle.

"Thanks."

They both sat down and put on their shoes before picking out their bowling balls. Being petite, it took Danielle a little longer to find something to feel comfortable for her to hold.

"Do you need the bumper rails?" he asked.

She glared at him. "No. I do not. I'm not *that* bad."

As they played the first game, it was very apparent to Danielle that she really was *that* bad. Bennett played like he was on a bowling league, and she played like she actually did need bumper rails and possibly eyeglasses.

When they finished the first game, Bennett had nachos and a large pepperoni pizza delivered to their table, along with a pitcher of soda.

"I feel like I'm on a date in high school," Danielle said, laughing.

"I just thought it would be fun to do something a lot more casual tonight. I hope you're having a good time."

She smiled. "I always have fun when I'm with you, Bennett."

He leaned across the table and gave her a quick kiss before grabbing a nacho covered in a huge mound of cheese and popping it into his mouth. She'd never seen him so at ease.

"And I always have fun with you. I think things are going pretty well, don't you?"

"So far."

"Do you ever just relax?"

She shrugged her shoulders. "This is how I act when I'm relaxed."

They finished eating and played another game, with Bennett beating her yet again. She had to think of something that she did better than him, so that her pride wasn't completely obliterated.

"What if I cook dinner for you at your house tomorrow night?"

"Oh, that sounds nice. To what do I owe the pleasure?"

"Well, a little birdie told me it's your birthday tomorrow. Why didn't you tell me?"

"Who let that slip?"

"I'll never reveal my sources," she said, knowing full well that both Morty and Naomi had told her.

"I'm not big on celebrating my birthday."

"Why is that?"

"When I was a kid, it just wasn't a big deal. We didn't have enough money to have birthday parties. Usually, my mom would take me to the local thrift store and just let me pick something out. I would almost always get a book."

"You know, you're not that little boy anymore, Bennett. You deserve to be celebrated. So I'm going to make you my famous Chicago deep dish lasagna with extra cheese and a secret ingredient."

"Oh, is that so?"

She grinned. "Trust me, you've never had anything like it. I'm also going to make my special garlic knots."

"Well, how can I possibly say no to all of that?"

"You can't. I'll come over at five o'clock to start cooking?"

"You can come over whenever you want," he said, running his finger across her cheek.

"Your boss?" Danielle's mother said from the other end of the phone.

"Yes, mother."

"Do you think that's wise, Danielle?"

"We're just seeing how it goes, Mom. It's no big deal."

"It is a big deal. Your career has already been so destroyed."

"What happened to that very positive, proud mother I talked to on the phone the last time?"

Her mother sighed. "I'm trying to be positive. I am proud of you. I just don't want to see you get your heart broken all over again."

"How will I ever meet someone if I'm too scared to see what happens?"

"I want you to meet someone. I just don't want it to be your boss!"

"Mom, at some point you have to let go. You must realize that I'm almost forty years old, and I can make my own decisions. I just need you to be there to support me. Okay?"

"I'm sorry. You're right. You're totally right. I used to hate when my mother would meddle in my business, and I'm doing it to you. I promise not to do it again."

"Thank you. Now, tell me how things are going in your life."

For the next half hour, her mother regaled her with tales of research and germs and her new boyfriend. When they hung up, Danielle laid back in her chair and smiled. Tonight was the night she would celebrate Bennett's birthday, and she was looking forward to it.

Things were finally going well. She liked her job. She liked the residents. She liked Bennett. Maybe more than liked.

Of course, he had no idea what she had planned for his birthday. It would definitely be a night he would always remember.

∼

"Oh, no!"

"What's wrong?"

"You don't have any oregano."

"I don't? I thought I did…" He rummaged through the pantry and several cabinets before giving up. "I don't understand where it could've gone."

Of course, he had no idea that she had stashed it away in her purse as soon as she had gotten there. It was all part of her plan.

"I don't suppose you could run to the grocery store and get some? Otherwise, the meal will be ruined."

He smiled, slid his hands around her waist, and kissed her neck. "You don't have to go to all this trouble. We can just go out to dinner."

"Bennett, I've been excited about this all day. Please, just run to the store?" She looked up at him, batting her eyelashes.

He groaned and then laughed, pinching her on the side. "Fine. I'll run to the store so that you can make me this masterpiece of food, but only because you're so dang cute."

Danielle watched him take his keys and walk out the front door. She peered out the window until he was out of sight before running out the back door. Beside the deck stood about twenty very hot residents, all of whom she had invited to the birthday party. They were the people Bennett was the closest to, including Morty, of course.

"I'm so sorry for keeping you waiting. It took me forever to get him out of the house. Come on in!"

She led them all to the back guest room and instructed them to be very quiet. Bennett would only be gone for about ten minutes, since the grocery store was very close to his house.

Danielle also ran out into the living room and quickly started hanging up all the decorations she had hidden in a trunk he kept beside the sofa. By the time she was finished, sweat was running down her back from nervousness and activity.

As if on cue, she heard him putting the key in the lock, and she stood back, a smile on her face. When Bennett walked through the door, he saw all the decorations.

"What on earth?"

"Happy birthday!" She yelled loudly, causing all the residents to come storming out of the guest room yelling surprise. Bennett held his hand to his chest and started laughing. He definitely had no idea what was going on.

"Oh, my gosh! You guys almost gave me a heart attack!"

Everybody laughed and the next couple of hours were spent celebrating Bennett. Danielle had never seen him smile so much, and it made her feel good to have done that for him.

They had catering brought in from the diner, and everybody sat on the sofa, at the table and even out on the deck. It felt good to have a house filled with laughter.

"Thank you so much for doing this. I've never had a birthday party," Bennett said, as they watched the last person leave.

"You've never had a birthday party?" she asked, her eyes wide.

"Never. Once I could afford it, I certainly didn't see a need to throw a party for myself. I'm not that vain."

"I feel so honored to have thrown you your first birthday party. And I was able to surprise you!"

He pulled her into a tight embrace and pressed his lips to the top of her head. "You have definitely surprised me, Danielle Wright."

As the evening wound down, Danielle and Bennett sat on the deck, staring out into the dark ocean, listening to the waves. She loved how he pulled their chairs closer together and held her hand, as if he was afraid she was going to vanish.

She was dozing off when her phone vibrated in her pocket. With her mother being alone in the city, she often worried that something may have happened to her, so she had started answering the phone no matter what number came up.

"I should take this."

Bennett stood up. "No problem. I'll open a bottle of wine."

He walked into the house, sliding the door partially closed behind him.

"Hello?"

"Danielle? It's so good to hear your voice."

It took her a moment to place who she was talking to, but then she realized it was Robert LaRusse, her old boss at the hospital.

"Mr. LaRusse?"

"I've told you a million times to call me Robert. How are you doing?"

"I am doing well," she stammered, still confused as to why he was calling her. She had found out weeks ago that her job had been filled, so there was no reason for him to be calling her now.

"Listen, I won't keep you long. I'm calling to beg you."

"Beg me?"

"Listen, Danielle, you're the best ICU nurse I've ever seen. So quick on your feet, innovative, empathetic with the patients and their families. Your organizational and leadership skills are second to none."

"Well, thank you for the compliments. I'm curious as to why you're calling me?"

"I want you back."

She stood there, her eyes wide as she stared out at the ocean in front of her. "I don't know what to say. I thought you already filled my position?"

He sighed loud enough for her to hear. "We did. It's been a fiasco. I swear, I don't know where this woman was trained, but she's terrible. She can't lead the staff. Everything is so disorganized now."

"I'm sorry to hear that."

"I've heard a bit about what you're doing at your new job. I think we can both agree that you were meant for more. There's no way they're paying you what I could, and you can't be professionally fulfilled there."

She laughed under her breath. "You'd be surprised."

"Look, I'm going to text you a number. A salary. I want you to take a look at it and then call me as soon as you've decided. I have to do something soon because this woman isn't running things well. I would like to think that I could get you to come back. Richard is gone now, and everybody here misses you. Nobody thinks badly of you, Danielle."

"I'm very flattered, but…" Just as she was about to finish her sentence, a text message from him came through with the salary being offered. Her eyes almost popped out of her head when she realized it was almost double what she had been making.

"From your silence, I take it that you just received my text?"

"But… How can you…"

"I know it's a lot more than you were making, but I went to the board and I fought for you. If we hire somebody else, they won't be making nearly that much. If you come back, we're willing to pay you almost double your previous salary."

She stood there, stunned, staring at her phone screen like it was in another language.

"I… I need some time…"

"I totally understand. You moved your life all the way to an island in South Carolina. It'll take time to get everything moved back here so that you're ready to get started."

"Can I call you later? I'm kind of in the middle of something right now," she said, turning around to make sure that Bennett wasn't behind her.

"Of course. We'll talk soon."

She ended the call, slipped her phone in her pocket and tried to catch her breath. Double her salary? That would be life-changing. She had already made a great salary, but she could save so much for her future and her retirement if she went back.

There was a part of her that longed for the familiarity, but there was a growing part of her that was feeling more at home on Wisteria Island. She didn't know what to do.

"Is everything okay?" Bennett asked, stepping out of the house. For a moment, she wondered if he had overheard any of her conversation.

"Oh, it's fine. It was just an old friend. Are you going to pour me a glass of that wine or what?"

CHAPTER 15

*B*ennett sat at his desk, staring at the work stacked up before him. He had done nothing constructive today at all. He just kept replaying the phone call he overheard Danielle having the night before. She had no idea he'd heard the whole thing.

He was so conflicted. She had thrown him the most wonderful birthday party, surprising him and making sure that he felt special. He was having a hard time balancing that with the fact that she seemed to be interested in taking her old job back.

It stirred up emotions that caused him to feel like he would never be enough for any woman. Like no one would ever really love him for who he was, at least not enough to stay.

"Bennett? You have a call on line two," Naomi said, over the intercom.

"Tell them I'm busy."

"This guy is very determined. He's been calling all

morning."

He signed. "Fine. I'll take it." He pressed the button for line two. "This is Bennett. How can I help you?"

"This is Dr. Richard Abernathy."

There was a long pause as Bennett sat there, trying to figure out if he was supposed to recognize the name. "Okay. Have we met?"

"No, but I think you've met my fiancé, Danielle."

Richard. *That* Richard.

Bennett's stomach twisted into a knot. He'd never wanted to reach through the phone and ring somebody's neck as much as he did right now. This guy even sounded like a jerk.

"Oh, Richard. Why are you calling me?"

"Look, I want to talk man-to-man. I understand you might be dating Danielle."

"And that is none of your business."

"I still care about Danielle. I still love her."

"Well, dude, I don't think she feels the same."

"Probably not. I really screwed up. I'm man enough to admit that."

"I think you might need to call Dr. Phil. You have the wrong number."

"Listen, you can't let her lose her whole career."

"What on earth are you talking about?"

"They've offered her her old job back at double the salary. Even though I know she'll never be with me again, and I don't even work at that hospital anymore, I want to see her do well. I care enough to try to get you to understand that she needs to go back. She needs to go back to her old life. You didn't know her then, but she was a force."

"She's a grown woman. She makes her own decisions. I'm not keeping her here."

"Danielle is looking for love. She's looking for comfort because of what I did. She's on the rebound. You have to know that, man."

"She's not on the rebound. We have something special, and I'm not pushing her to do anything."

"Just think about it. Is she going to look at you one day and be resentful because she lost everything she built? Double her salary. That's what they're offering her. Can you offer her an opportunity like that?"

Bennett paused for a moment. He could never offer her anything close to the challenge that being an ICU nurse would. He knew that. Danielle knew that. Was he holding her back? Sure, he could match the salary, but would she be fulfilled on Wisteria Island for the rest of her career?

"Again, this is none of your business," Bennett said in a monotone voice.

"You're probably right. Let me just say one more thing. She's the most loyal woman you'll ever meet. She will never leave that island if she's dating you. You have to decide what's best for her and care enough about her to make sure it happens."

"You mean manipulate the situation?"

"Call it what you will. I wish I had done things differently. I only cared about myself, and then I lost everything. I just want to make sure that Danielle doesn't pay for everything I did."

"Well, too late," Bennett said, hanging up the phone.

$\sim$

DANIELLE WAS LOOKING FORWARD to another evening with Bennett. They were supposed to go to dinner over on the mainland, and he was picking her up in half an hour. She couldn't wait to see him, as he was the highlight at the end of each of her days.

She hated to admit that she was looking so forward to it. Part of her felt like she was weak and too vulnerable, but she also felt very stable in this new relationship. There was just something about Bennett that made her feel like a whole different life was possible.

Her phone rang on the counter, almost vibrating its way off the edge where she had it charging. She ran over to catch it on the third ring before it went to voicemail.

"Hello?"

"Hey."

"Bennett. I was looking out the window to make sure you hadn't arrived early. I'm all dressed and ready to go!"

He cleared his throat. "Listen, I'm kind of tied up here at the office tonight. I hate to cancel at the last minute, but maybe we can do it another time?"

She immediately felt let down, but things happened. People got stuck at work all the time. It was a little odd that Bennett did, since he had total control over his schedule, but she had been keeping him away from the office a lot more recently. It was likely that his work really was backing up.

"Of course! I totally understand being busy at work. I'll tell you what. I'll go pick up some food from the diner and bring it over. We can have a little picnic at your office!"

"No. Thank you. I just really need to focus so I'm going to eat a snack out of the vending machine and just keep moving forward."

She paused for a moment. "Bennett, is everything all right?"

"Yeah. Totally fine. I'm just really tired."

He said nothing else, and there was just an awkward silence that hung between them. "Well, okay then. I guess I'll talk to you tomorrow?"

"Sure. We'll play it by ear."

Before she could say anything else, he ended the call. Something had been terribly wrong in his voice. She thought for a moment about going to his office anyway, seeing him face-to-face and trying to figure out what was going on. She would not do that. He obviously wanted some space from her for some reason, and it made her nervous. Opening her heart again had been one of the most difficult things she'd ever done in her life. She certainly didn't want to pursue somebody if they weren't interested in her.

Feeling defeated, she went to the kitchen and pulled left over chicken out of the refrigerator. She put a piece on a plate and popped it into the microwave before digging a bag of chips out of the pantry. It wouldn't be the world's best dinner, but at least she wouldn't starve to death.

"YOU CANCELED YOUR DATE?" Morty asked, standing there with his hands on his hips.

"I didn't know what else to do."

Bennett sat at Morty's kitchen table, a place he often went when he just needed some time to get away from all the other residents. Morty was crazy all by himself, but he was a fun kind of crazy.

"She's a wonderful gal, Bennett. You can't let her go."

"I know that. I am head over heels for her. I can't get around the fact that I might be keeping her from something big."

Morty sat down across from him, reached over, and squeezed his hands. "She might be the one. She's worth fighting for."

"If it was about fighting another man, I would do it in a heartbeat. What if I'm keeping her from going back to the hospital and making double her salary?"

"You can easily pay her the same, I'm sure."

"It's not just about the money. She loved her job, and I could hear how interested she was when she got that call. She didn't say no."

"Then talk to her. Ask her about the phone call."

"I can't put her on the spot like that. She's obviously thinking of going back, and maybe she won't even tell me the truth. Maybe she won't want to hurt my feelings."

"So you're just going to let her go?"

"I don't know what I'm going to do, but I do know that continuing to deepen our relationship is only going to hurt both of us."

"Oh, Bennett, I think you're making a mistake. Sometimes a genuine love only comes once in a lifetime. I don't want to see you let yours go."

"If I love her, and I think I do, letting her go might be the most loving thing I've ever done."

DANIELLE STOOD in the doorway of the waiting room, staring out onto the street at everybody walking by. A part of her hoped she would catch a glimpse of Bennett, that he would come into her office and explain why he'd been avoiding her for the last few days.

She had tried to call him one time, but she wasn't a desperate woman. She certainly would not chase anyone. She had been there, done that, and never wanted to do it again.

This was why romance wasn't worth it to her. There weren't these big happy endings like she saw in romantic movies or books. There were no soulmates. Soulmates didn't do this kind of thing to each other.

"Oh, hey, Gladys. I'm so glad to see you today."

She tried to sound excited as Gladys came in for her follow up appointment. Gladys had been trying new medication since they met with the neurologist a few weeks back.

Danielle was eager to see about any progress she'd made, and at least it would give her a great distraction from her personal life.

"You look terrible!" Gladys said. One thing was for sure, she hadn't lost her ability to say whatever was on her mind.

Danielle laughed. "It's been a rough few days. Why don't you come on back?"

Danielle walked back to one of the exam rooms and Gladys followed her, popping herself up onto the examination table. She swung her legs back-and-forth like a little kid as they dangled over the edge.

"What's the matter?"

"Why don't we just talk about your medical situation?"

"I thought we were friends."

Danielle looked at her. "We are friends, Gladys."

"Well, friends tell friends why they look terrible."

Danielle laughed. "Fine. I was dating a guy, and he started pulling away and making excuses for not seeing me. So, I'm really confused and a little sad."

"You mean Bennett?"

"How did you know that?"

"Everybody knows that!" she said, waving her hand in Danielle's direction. "We all know about you two kissing on the beach."

Danielle rolled her eyes. "Morty cannot keep a secret."

"Well, I could've told you that."

"Now, tell me about you. How's it going with the new medications?"

"Good. I haven't seen any aliens since I started them. I haven't been getting confused at all."

"That's fantastic, Gladys!"

"Yeah, and I called that niece of mine and set her straight. When we were finished, she was very assured that I am in my right mind."

"I'm so happy for you."

"Listen, I might seem like an old lady who knows nothing, but I've been in love before. You shouldn't let Bennett slip away. Something must be wrong. He's not that kind of man."

"Well, I thought so too. But it turns out that he is."

She didn't want to believe it, but maybe Bennett was just like all the others that she'd dated in her lifetime. He was interested for a while, and then he just disappeared out of her life. They always let her down in one way or another.

Bennett hated grocery shopping, especially when he knew whatever he was buying was only going to be cooked for one. He missed Danielle with every fiber of his being. Yet he had done everything to avoid her for days. It seemed so childish and immature, but his heart couldn't take looking into her soft brown eyes and making up yet another lie.

He knew he had to be hurting her, but he thought it was for the best in the long run. This morning, when he had put up the new ad for an island nurse, he didn't even want to hit submit. He knew what was coming.

She was definitely going to quit, and he couldn't be left in the lurch when she did.

The opportunity at the hospital was just too big. He had done a lot of research, even calling a friend of his who'd worked at that hospital, to find out just what an opportunity it was. He couldn't let her miss out on that. And they were only holding her job for a short period of time.

He didn't want her to go. If he had his wish, she would stay on that island with him forever. They would raise a brood of old people together. What he wanted wasn't what was best for her.

He reached up and got a box of macaroni and cheese. Again, not a very mature thing to eat, but something that was quick and easy for a single man.

He would always be a single man. There was nobody that had wanted to live with him on Wisteria Island except for Danielle. His soulmate. He truly believed that. He would just get older and older until he moved into one of the cottages and started square dancing.

He turned the corner to go down the cereal aisle and ran his cart right into someone else's.

"Oh, sorry about that…" He looked up and locked eyes with Danielle.

"Bennett." She said it in a matter-of-fact way. Gone were the soft features of her face, looking at him on the beach. In place of that was a woman who was harshly looking at him like she wanted to be anywhere but there.

"I was going to call you today."

"Were you? That would be unusual."

"I am sorry I've been a little distant lately."

"Oh, have you? I hadn't noticed," she said, dryly. She wouldn't make eye contact.

"I just think that maybe things were moving a little too fast for me..." He was completely lying, of course. He hadn't expected to run into her, and thinking on his feet wasn't one of his strong suits.

"Yeah, I feel pretty much the same way."

She did? That was news to him. Maybe she had already decided to leave the island, and she wasn't as attached to him as he had assumed.

"Okay. So we'll just go back to being friends?"

"I think it's better if we just go back to being coworkers."

"Right. Okay. If that's what you want."

"I think that's what you want, Bennett," she said, looking away and pushing her cart down the aisle. As he watched her leave, he felt like he was going to throw up. He had finally found the right woman for him, and he was letting her go. It just seemed wrong on so many levels.

~

"You already broke up?" her mother said, shock in her voice. "But I thought everything was going so great?"

"I did too. I haven't ever felt like that about anyone, and it was like a light switch flipped. Everything was going great. We were getting closer, and it really seemed like this was turning into something serious and long-term. I could see a future with Bennett."

"What do you think happened?"

"I really don't know. One day everything was fine, the next day he just wanted to be friends again. I will not beg a man to be with me."

"Of course not. So what are you going to do now?"

"I don't know. I like my job here, and I would like to stay. I never thought I'd hear myself say that."

Her mother laughed. "Me either. I want you to be happy, Danielle. If that job makes you happy, don't let some man take that away from you yet again."

"I just don't know if it's going to be too uncomfortable to continue working here."

"Take it day by day. Don't decide right now. Just let this settle down for a bit and see how you feel. Focus on your patients."

It was all good advice. She knew her mother was right, but would her heart be able to take seeing Bennett all the time? It wasn't like she could get away from him. He owned the island, and he was extremely involved.

"Well, I'd better go. I have a patient coming in shortly."

"You're going to be okay. Everything happens for a reason."

"Do you really believe that, Mom?"

"I do. I've got the benefit of a few decades more experience than you do, honey. One day you'll look back on all of this and realize it was worth it. It happened for some special reason."

"I sure hope you're right."

~

BENNETT SIFTED through the resumes that had already come in through the online job system. None of these nurses appealed to him. They didn't have the length of experience that Danielle had, and they all just seemed dull and boring.

Of course, maybe he needed a dull and boring nurse that wouldn't attract his attention at all. Maybe she needed to have a giant wart on the end of her nose so that he wouldn't even look her way. Not that he had been in the habit of dating the other nurses he'd hired. It had only been Danielle because she was the special one.

It had been days since they ran into each other in the grocery store. A part of him wanted to just jump on the golf cart, go straight to her cottage and apologize for the way he'd been acting. He wanted to explain himself. He didn't want her to stay because of him. He wanted her to stay because that's what she wanted to do.

Morty had driven him crazy, trying to get him to tell Danielle the truth. Tell her what he overheard and about the phone call from Richard. Bennett refused, and he swore Morty to secrecy.

Every day, he expected to get a note from Danielle saying that she was giving her notice. As each day passed, he grew more and more surprised that she hadn't said anything. Surely she had missed the deadline to go back to her old job. Why wasn't she leaving?

He didn't know what to do. It felt like a standoff, and he was just waiting for the inevitable shoe to drop. It made no sense that she would stay. Ever since the day she arrived on the island, she had tried to leave. He had forced her hand over and over, literally manipulating her into staying. Begging, pleading, reasoning. At least that's how he felt now.

But now he knew he loved her. He would not force her to stay. So, he would continue doing what he had been doing – waiting. Waiting for her to make the ultimate decision. Waiting for his heart to completely break in half.

∽

"Hello?"

"Hey, Danielle! It's Carla."

She hadn't heard from Carla in a couple of months, so she was quite surprised to hear from her now.

"Hi. What's going on?"

"LaRusse said that he talked to you recently about coming back? Have you made a decision yet?"

"Did he ask you to call me?"

"No. I'm just really anxious to have you back. This woman he hired is terrible. Nobody will listen to her like they did with you. Plus, she's a disorganized mess!"

"That's what I've heard. And no, I haven't decided yet. Things are a little up in the air here."

"Oh. I guess I misunderstood."

"Misunderstood what?"

"Well, as LaRusse was looking to put up an ad for the job in case you decided not to come back, he saw an ad... for Wisteria Island."

"What?"

"Yeah, some guy named Bennett was looking for a new nurse for the island."

"That can't be right. It's probably just the old ad."

"No, it was just put up a few days ago."

Danielle's stomach twisted into a knot. "Carla, I have to go. I'll call you later, okay?"

She didn't wait for Carla to respond and pressed end on the phone. She ran across the room to her laptop, opened it up and started searching on the nurse jobs website. Sure enough, it didn't take her very long to find the posting.

Why was Bennett looking for a new nurse? Was he about to fire her? She wasn't going to give him that opportunity. There was no way she was going to let him win.

CHAPTER 16

*D*anielle stood on the other side of the door, her knuckles poised over the wood, ready to knock. She stopped for a moment, clutching the piece of paper in her hand as she took another deep breath.

This was a big deal. This was going to mean the end of something she thought would last a long time. This was going to be another failed attempt at starting a new life. Like it or not, some of her hopes and dreams were on the other side of that door, and she was going to be saying goodbye to a lot of them.

Goodbye to Bennett. Goodbye to Wisteria Island. Goodbye to all the residents who had finally accepted her. She loved those people like family.

Steeling herself once again, she knocked on the door.

"Come in, Naomi." Hearing Bennett's voice made her insides twist and turn like one of those scary looking roller coasters at an amusement park.

She slowly opened the door, revealing to Bennett that she was not Naomi.

"Hi."

"Danielle, I didn't know you were coming."

"I never thought I'd be standing here, either."

"Please, have a seat."

She closed the door behind her, wanting privacy for some reason. Slowly, she made her way to the chair across from his desk and sat down. The awkwardness that hung between them was such a stark contrast to the relationship they had been building just a couple of weeks ago.

"So, why are you here?"

Using all the courage she currently had in her body, she slid the piece of paper across the desk. "I'm putting in my notice."

He blew out a breath and nodded his head, but he didn't seem to be very surprised. "I've been expecting this."

"Well, I like to live up to expectations," she said dryly.

"You're the best nurse we've ever had."

"Then do you care to explain why you started running an advertisement for my job before I even quit?"

"I just knew when things broke down between us, you would probably be leaving. I didn't want to be caught with my pants down, so to speak. You know how much the residents depend on medical care."

"So you thought I was so immature that I would

quit my job and leave these people in the lurch because you didn't want to date anymore?"

"That's not what I'm saying at all…"

"Look, there's no need to prolong this. I'm giving you two weeks' notice because that's what I think is the right thing to do. I hope that gives you plenty of time to find someone new."

He sighed. "I haven't even started interviewing anyone. Nobody seems to be the right fit."

"Do you really need two weeks' notice? Maybe you could borrow a nurse from the doctor's office on the mainland for a couple of weeks."

"I suppose I could do that. I'm sure you're eager to get back to your life."

She thought that was a strange thing for him to say, given that she hadn't mentioned going back to her life. In fact, she had no plans to pick up where she left off. She was still aching for something new, and she would likely go some place where nobody knew her. Start over *again*. Keep hoping for a new life.

"Great. I'll talk to Jeremy about moving me over to the mainland tomorrow."

"Tomorrow?"

"I've already seen most of my patients this week to make sure that they are set for a while. Gladys is doing well, and Dorothy had a couple of sessions with the psychiatrist. She's doing well on her new medication. There's really nothing else I need to do here, so another nurse should be able to step in temporarily."

"You did such a great job. I'm sorry to see you go."

"Are you really?"

He looked at her with such a sadness on his face that she couldn't place. It felt like there was some piece of the puzzle she was missing, but it was obvious that Bennett would not tell her what it was.

"Danielle, you have no idea how painful this is for me."

"I feel like I don't understand you at all. You have one last chance right now to tell me what's going on. Why are you pushing me away like this?"

He turned and looked out the window, sucked in a breath, and then blew it out before speaking.

"There's nothing I'm hiding. I wish you nothing but the best, Danielle. I'm always here to provide a great reference if you need it."

She sat there quietly for a moment, staring at him, waiting for him to snap out of it. But he didn't. He just looked down at his papers until she finally left the room.

As Danielle walked out of the building and back out onto the sidewalk, her eyes filled with tears. Never did she think she would already miss this place, these people. She had eased into her new life, and she didn't want to let it go. She loved her cottage, the view of the ocean, and the routine of living on Wisteria Island.

But tomorrow was a new day, and it wasn't one she was looking forward to.

~

BENNETT HADN'T SLEPT all night. He couldn't believe he was willingly letting her go, but it still seemed like the right thing to do. When she had asked why he was pushing her away, he had a chance to tell her he overheard the call, but he didn't do it.

As he sat on his deck, drinking a cup of coffee and staring out at the water, he wondered what life was going to be like on the island once Danielle was gone.

Jeremy told him she was leaving this morning and that her bags had already been packed. She had given her keys to Eddie and was headed to the boat the last time he heard. Sounded like she was anxious to get back to her old life and her doubled salary.

As he was getting up to get another cup of coffee, his cell phone rang on the table beside him.

"Bennett Alexander."

"Ah, the infamous Bennett Alexander. I thought I'd never reach you," a woman said. He didn't recognize her voice, but she didn't sound pleased with him at all.

"And who is this?"

"This is Danielle's mother."

Now he was really confused. What on earth would Danielle's mother want with him?

"I think you might be looking for Danielle. She should have her cell phone with her…"

"No, I'm looking for you. I want to know what kind of man could break my daughter's heart like this knowing what she's already been through?"

"I'm not following."

"You broke up with her, didn't you?"

"I think it was more of a mutual thing."

"You gave her job away right from under her!"

"Look, ma'am, you may not know that she's going to take her old job back at double the salary."

"No, she's not! They offered it to her, but she turned it down weeks ago."

"What?"

"She turned it down. And you still broke her heart and put an ad up for her job before she even gave notice. What kind of jerk are you?"

He sat there frozen, his heart pounding, unable to draw a breath. "A big one, apparently."

"What?"

"Look, I hate to rush you off the phone, but there's something I have to do!" he said, ending the call and running around the side of his house.

When he got out to the sidewalk, he saw Morty walking his dog."Where are you going with your pants on fire?"

"I have to find Danielle! I misunderstood. She wasn't going to take that job. She turned it down, and I didn't know!"

He ran straight down the sidewalk toward the dock, with Morty calling behind him. "Run faster!"

The island wasn't that big, but right now it seemed like there were five-hundred miles between them. He didn't know how to get there any faster than his legs were currently carrying him.

As he ran, residents followed him like in that scene from Forrest Gump. They weren't quick, but they were coming out in force. Then he saw Morty with his little dog riding in the golf cart as fast as he could down the center of the street.

"Get on!" he said as he pulled up next to Bennett.

Bennett jumped inside without saying a word, just pointing toward the dock.

Morty was driving like a racecar driver, and he was terrified they were going to flip over at any moment. When they finally rounded the corner, he saw Danielle's boat pulling away from the dock.

"Wait! Wait!" he yelled, waving his arms like a lunatic.

Danielle was looking the other direction and couldn't hear him over the boat motor.

"Jeremy! Stop the boat!"

Finally, Jeremy saw him and turned off the boat, squinting his eyes as he looked toward the shore. Bennett turned around to see at least thirty residents standing there with him, obviously showing moral support. Everybody from Gladys to Dorothy Monroe to Frank were standing there helping him wave, trying to get Danielle's attention.

Jeremy started the motor and moved back toward the dock.

"What's up, boss?"

Danielle finally turned around and realized what was happening. She looked dumbfounded as all the residents were waving their hands at her and yelling.

"I need to talk to Danielle."

"Bennett, I have nothing to say. Why are you doing this?"

"Please. Just two minutes of your time."

Jeremy looked at her, and she finally nodded her head. He helped her out of the boat and onto the dock.

Bennett turned around and looked at the crowd. "Give us a little space, guys."

They backed up a few feet, and Bennett looked back at Danielle.

"What's going on?"

"I didn't know."

"You didn't know what?"

"I didn't know that you didn't take the job."

She stared at him. "How did you even know about the job?"

"I overheard your phone call."

"What? Why didn't you just tell me that?"

"I was trying to decide what to do about it when Richard called me."

Her jaw clenched. "Richard called you? What did he say?"

"He said that if I kept you from taking that job, I was going to ruin your life. All I really want for you is a great life, Danielle. So I thought if I gave you up, I was actually showing how much I care about you."

"So you overheard my call, talked to Richard on the phone and then put a job posting up all without telling me?"

"When you put it that way, it sounds ridiculous, but I thought I was doing the right thing."

"I don't get it. Then why run all the way over here on the dock and stop me from leaving if you thought I was going onto my new improved life?"

"Because your mom called me."

Her eyes almost popped out of her head. "My mom? Why is all of this going on behind my back?"

"She called to yell at me because she said I broke your heart. Then she told me you weren't taking that job."

"Well, she was right about both of those things."

"So where were you going?"

"I don't know. I was going to go rent a hotel room and look for a new job in a different state. I had no plans to go back to that hospital, no matter how much they paid me. I didn't want to leave Wisteria Island."

"You didn't?"

"No. This place grew on me a long time ago. I thought we were building something which gave me another reason to stay."

"Is there any chance we can still build something?"

She shrugged her shoulders. "Can you promise not to keep things from me and always tell me the truth?"

"Yes, I can. I will never make that mistake again."

"I'm sorry I didn't tell you about the job offer. I was never really considering it, so I didn't think I needed to bring it up."

"I shouldn't have been eavesdropping on your conversation, so there's nothing for you to apologize for, Danielle."

"I have to know I can trust you, Bennett. I've already been with a man who kept things from me."

He reached down and took both of her hands in his. "I promise you can trust me. I have about thirty-something people over here who will hit me on the head with canes and walkers and scooters if I ever do anything to hurt you."

She laughed. "Then can I please have my job back?"

"You can have whatever you want because I love you, Danielle Wright. Turns out you're my Miss Wright."

"And I love you too, even though that is the corniest thing I've ever heard anyone say," she said, rising up on her tiptoes to pull him into a kiss. As they stood there on the dock, lips pressed together, a rousing roar of applause and hoots emanated from the quirky cast of characters that they called family.

Find ALL of Rachel's books at www.RachelHannaAuthor.com!

Made in United States
North Haven, CT
18 March 2022

17286465R00143

WISTERIA ISLAND

RACHEL HANNA